The Man Was Practically Naked.

Silvery streams of water ran over his tanned flesh, making him look slick and smooth. His swimsuit was a tiny strip of electric blue that didn't so much hide as accentuate. His thighs were thick and strong and covered with dark hair. He was like some erotic dream of a lover one might conjure up on a lazy summer afternoon. But he was much too real.

"Talk fast," she said breathlessly, trying to still her pounding heart. "I'm in a hurry."

His eyebrows rose, and his hands went to his hips. "Is it just me?" he asked. "Or are you this rude to all the men you know?"

She flushed. No one had accused her being rude since she was six years old and refused to kiss Aunt Lulu goodbye. But she knew he was absolutely right. "I'm sorry," she said. "I guess I tend to forget my manners when I'm upset."

"What have I done to upset you?" he asked quietly.

What a question! In exasperation, she said, "Do you ever appear anywhere fully dressed?"

"Not if I can help it. I'm a nature freak. How about you?"

She shook her head. "I think nature is best tamed," she asserted. "Like you ought to be."

Dear Reader:

Spring is in the air! Birds are singing, flowers are blooming and thoughts are turning to love. Since springtime is such a romantic time, I'm happy to say that April's Silhouette Desires are the very essence of romance.

Now we didn't exactly plan it this way, but three of our books this month are connecting stories. *The Hidden Pearl* by Celeste Hamilton is part of **Aunt Eugenia's Treasures**. *Ladies' Man* by Raye Morgan ties into *Husband for Hire* (#434). And our *Man of the Month*, Garret Cagan in Ann Major's *Scandal's Child* ties into her successful **Children of Destiny** series.

I know many of you love connecting stories, but if you haven't read the ''prequels'' and spin-offs, please remember that each and every Silhouette Desire is a wonderful love story in its own right.

And don't miss our other April books: *King of the Mountain* by Joyce Thies, *Guilty Secrets* by Laura Leone and *Sunshine* by Jo Ann Algermissen!

Before I go, I have to say that I'd love to know what you think about our new covers. Please write in and let me know. I'm always curious about what the readers think—and I also believe that your thoughts are important.

Until next month,

Lucia Macro
Senior Editor

RAYE
MORGAN

LADIES' MAN

SILHOUETTE *Desire*

Published by Silhouette Books New York

America's Publisher of Contemporary Romance

SILHOUETTE BOOKS
300 East 42nd St., New York, N.Y. 10017

ISBN: 0-373-05562-5

First Silhouette Books printing April 1990

Printed in the U.S.A.

Books by Raye Morgan

Silhouette Romance

Roses Never Fade #427

Silhouette Desire

Embers of the Sun #52
Summer Wind #101
Crystal Blue Horizon #141
A Lucky Streak #393
Husband for Hire #434
Too Many Babies #543
Ladies' Man #562

RAYE MORGAN

favors settings in the West, which is where she has spent most of her life. She admits to a penchant for western heroes, believing that whether he's a rugged outdoorsman or a smooth city sophisticate he tends to have a streak of wildness that the romantic heroine can't resist taming. She's been married to one of those western men for twenty years and is busy raising four more in her Southern California home.

One

―――

Guess what. I think Mom's having an affair.''

Trish blinked, her heart doing a quick flip-flop, and then shook her head and laughed. "You crazy person," she chided her sister affectionately. She shifted the receiver of the telephone to her "talking" ear, hunching one shoulder to hold it in place, and continued shuffling order forms at the same time. "Our mother doesn't have affairs. She's married to our father. Remember?"

She continued separating pink slips from blue slips and letting the yellow copies flutter toward the wastebasket. "Listen, Shelley, I'm really busy. The shop's been full of customers all day and I've got a rush order for personalized dinosaur stationery...."

"Forget the pterodactyls. I've seen the guy."

Trish sighed. When Shelley got this excited, it was best to let her get it out of her system before she did something rash. "Okay. Tell me all."

Shelley took a bite of a very juicy apple and the crunching sound came across the telephone loud and clear. "I hadn't talked to Mom since she got back from her latest ski trip to Mammoth so I thought I'd stop by her apartment and say hi."

Her apartment. Trish always winced when she heard those words. Her mother and father had been separated for six months now, but she still couldn't quite believe it was true. The thought of that big old house without her mother, of her father wandering those memory-filled halls all alone....it tore her heart out. But almost as bad was her mother living in that yuppified apartment like some latter-day bachelorette. Six months. She'd never thought the separation would last this long.

"So I rang the bell," Shelley continued, her narrative punctuated by the crisp sounds of apple munching. "And this man answered." She sighed heavily. "Trish, you wouldn't believe it. I mean, this guy was a hunk. I wish *I* could find someone this good-looking!"

Trish felt a tremor of unease, but she suppressed it with a shrug. "Shelley, just because some man was visiting Mom's apartment...."

"'Visiting' is hardly the word for it. Trish..." Her voice lowered to a conspiratorial tone. "Trish, he had his shirt off."

Trish blinked. Her attention was finally fully focused. She dropped the order forms and frowned. There had to be some explanation. "Maybe he...maybe he was working on the plumbing or...or inspecting for bugs...or..."

"Do those types usually take their shirts off at your place?"

"No," she admitted reluctantly, her fingers curling more tightly around the receiver, her heart beating just a little faster. "But . . . what did he say?"

"He said 'hello there' and gave me one of those toothy macho grins to die for and reached for his shirt. Which was on the floor, by the way," she added significantly.

Trish made a face at the far wall. This didn't make sense. Her parents might be separated, but it was surely a temporary situation. They were still definitely very married. The relationship between the two had always been volatile. Tam Becker wasn't the easiest man to live with. He was totally wrapped up in his business and that made her mother crazy sometimes. But she loved him. She had to. "Where was Mom?"

"Out. At least that was what he said." Shelley sighed. "He has this shaggy dark hair and these wide shoulders. . . ."

Trish frowned. "I don't get it."

"I told you. She's having an affair."

"No!" Trish rejected that theory out of hand, her heart beating hard at the thought. "There's got to be some good explanation."

Shelley's voice took on a new, careful note and all apple chewing ceased. "Trish, I think we're going to have to face facts. Mom has left Dad. This time, she's not going back."

Trish's free hand went to her short, copper-tipped hair, the fingers spiking through it in a gesture of denial. "Don't be silly. Of course she'll go back. She just needs some time. . . ."

"Trish, it's been six months. She's never left for more than a few days before. This time it's for real."

"No," Trish said huskily. "No, Shelley, I can't believe that. They are so perfect together. The two of them....they're like two halves of one whole. They're incomplete without each other." She had to swallow hard to get by the lump that was forming in her throat. "They belong together. It's...it's just not right for them to be apart."

For a moment neither one of them spoke. Trish took a deep breath. She was a big girl now, almost thirty, with her own life, her own business to run. She should be able to step aside and be objective about this whole thing. But somehow she couldn't. The thought of her parents permanently apart shook something fundamental in her. She refused to accept the possibility.

"Trish," Shelley ventured at last. "It's their life. Or lives, I guess I should say. And we really have no right to get involved."

Trish closed her eyes, hurting. "You know what I think?" she said quickly to her sister. "I have a feeling things will change Saturday, at the Spring Regatta. I know they'll both be there." Her voice lightened as she let her dream materialize. "She'll wear something white and filmy and he'll see her across the lawn and start walking toward her...."

"Maybe," Shelley interrupted. "Let's just hope she doesn't bring this guy along. That might put a bit of a crimp in your cheery little scenario."

Trish had to steady herself before speaking again. "Tell me more about this man in Mom's apartment," she said, her voice firm once more, but only with effort.

"What's to tell? He was gorgeous. Not handsome in the classical sense, but sexy, you know? Good body, clean hair, laughing eyes, and a look of...oh, I don't know...kind of the wanderlust sort. Does that make any sense?"

"A worthless charmer."

"You got it."

Trish's shoulders sagged. "We're making wild conjectures on very little evidence." She shook her head. "No, I just can't believe our mother would be having an affair with some stray...."

"Gorgeous."

"No-account..."

"Hunky."

"Gigolo..."

"Young."

"Young?" Trish swallowed.

"Well, younger than she is."

"How much younger?"

"Mid-thirties."

"Well that proves it. She's—"

"A beautiful, very well-preserved and youthful thinking forty-nine-year-old woman. A woman of style and grace and intelligence who any man over the age of consent would be proud to have on his arm."

Trish's mouth felt very dry. "True," she whispered. "True."

"You see?" Shelley crunched the apple again. "And as for me, I say more power to her. It's her life."

But she's our mother. Trish didn't say the words aloud. She was through arguing the point. Shelley didn't seem to understand just how important this was. She squared her shoulders. "I'm going over there to find out what's going on for myself."

"Right now?"

"Right now."

"But what about the pterodactyls?"

"They'll have to go into a holding pattern. I'll call you as soon as I get back."

She hung up the phone and sat still for a moment, gathering her emotional resources. Her cubbyhole of an office was her protected cave from the hustle and bustle of the shop. Order books and product samples spilled from every shelf in cheery disarray. Outside the door she could hear the low hum of voices.

Her shop, Paper Roses, was busy as usual. She'd opened her door two years before to almost instant success. Offering a unique selection of personalized stationery, cards and gift items, along with a staff of artists who decorated anything for a small added fee, the shop had become popular with young girls and their mothers, as well. It was an after-school hangout of sorts, a place where mothers met to compare notes and sip a cup of herbal tea or gourmet coffee in the back of the store while their daughters roamed the aisles, oohing and aahing over new purchases, stickers, ribbons, ink pads and rubber stamps. Paper Roses was her life, and she loved it. But she also loved her family. And she was ready to fight, if need be, to hold it together.

So, I guess it's time to circle the wagons, man the battle stations, call in the cavalry. She said aloud, "And meanwhile, I'm elected to go out on patrol...."

Laura Becker's new apartment was high above San Diego's Old Towne. Decorated in Nuevo-Mediterranean turquoises and pink against warm beige stucco, it looked very "now" and trendy. Everything that Trish's mother had never been until lately.

Trish hesitated when she saw that her mother's car was not in its accustomed spot in the parking area beneath the building. But that didn't necessarily mean that she was not at home. The car could be in the shop, or parked around the corner, or any of a number of possibilities. So she scuttled the momentary temptation to use that as an excuse to turn around and go home, steeled herself, and walked in past the still, blue pool, taking the stairs to the second floor.

Everything looked the same, felt the same, sounded the same. Nothing had changed. She began to relax. The whole thing was bound to turn out to be humbug. A sexy man in her mother's apartment! She grinned to herself, already enjoying how her mother would take the joke once she'd told her.

"That Shelley!" her mother would say. "What are we going to do with that child? She needs her wavelength adjusted or something. Why is it she always sees everything catty-corner from the way the rest of us do?"

Still grinning, Trish rapped sharply on the turquoise door.

"Just a minute," came the reply from inside. And the grin faded, because the voice was very masculine.

Trish held her breath, her pulse suddenly racing. It was true. There was a man in there where her mother ought to be. The door began to open and she stood very still, eyes wide.

He wasn't particularly tall, only about four inches taller than her five-foot-six height, but there was a sense of male substance to him, maybe because of the mass of well-developed muscles the open shirt displayed. The shirt was sea green, setting off the tan skin of his chest. The light covering of hair was brown black and concentrated around the dark nipples. His stone-washed jeans fit low on his hips, exposing his navel and the smooth ridges of muscle stretched taut across the curve of his pelvis. He was barefoot.

"Can I help you?"

The dark hair was too long and tipped here and there with sun streaks. The dark eyes were laughing as though she were doing something awfully amusing, and the set of his shoulders said, "Playboy" loud and clear. In one hand was a silver spoon, in the other a pint carton of ice cream. Butter brickle.

She stared at it. He bent down a bit to get his face back into her line of vision. "Can I help you?" he repeated.

Confusion poured through Trish. For a fleeting second she understood why Shelley had escaped as quickly as possible. But she couldn't do that. She had to see this through. She met his gaze and frowned, partly with worry, partly just to counter that laughter in his eyes.

"I'm looking for Laura Becker," she said, her voice shaking ever so slightly. "Is she here?"

He shook his head. "No."

Trish hesitated, then tried to look around him into the apartment. "She does still live here?" A sudden hope hit her. What if her mother had gone back home and hadn't wanted to tell anyone yet and she'd sublet her place to this....

"Yes, she still lives here," he said, dashing hopes helter-skelter. "She's just out right now."

Trish gathered all her strength and tried to look fierce, glaring into his casual gaze. "Who, exactly, are you?" she asked.

He grinned and Trish saw right away what Shelley had been talking about. The grin was lopsided and endearing and he scared her all the more by looking so damn adorable. "My name is Mason Ames," he said. "I'm sort of a friend of your mother's."

Trish's head snapped up and she searched his eyes. He was smiling and friendly, but she had no intention of being the same. "How did you know she was my mother?" she demanded. "I didn't say so."

"No," he admitted readily enough, seemingly amused by her attitude. "But she's got pictures of both daughters all over the place. I couldn't help but recognize you."

"Oh." All over the place? Trish's spirits sank even further. What was he doing "all over the place" in her mother's apartment?

The laughter had faded and he watched a bit uneasily as the various emotions chased themselves across her face. Apparently he hadn't expected the wariness she was exhibiting. When he glanced into the room, and then back out at her, it was evident to Trish that he wasn't sure what he wanted to do with her.

"Look," he said at last, "she should be back shortly. Do you want to come on in and wait for her?"

No. She wanted to run away as fast as she could. But she swallowed and set her shoulders. She had to do what had to be done. "Please," she said.

One masculine eyebrow rose at the tremor in her voice. She saw his reaction and steeled herself, brushing past him into the living room. The hysterical sounds of a game show came from the television set. A bottle of beer sat on her mother's rosewood coffee table. She glared at it, a fierce warning against making rings.

The room was decorated in warm colors, but somehow it had the temporary feeling of a motel room. The only personal items Trish saw were the photographs of Laura Becker's family that she had scattered everywhere, on the bookshelves, on the coffee table, hanging on the wall. There was a particularly engaging picture of Trish herself sitting near a window. Her face was tilted up toward the sun and she was laughing. Trish remembered the occasion. It had been her father's birthday two years before. The whole family had taken the yacht to Catalina for the weekend. The happiness of those days could be seen in Trish's face. She hated to think of what a picture taken today would show.

The man closed the door and came in behind her, hesitating only a moment before flopping down onto the couch. "Which one are you?" he asked, straining a bit, but managing to sound friendly. "Trish or Shelley?"

She paced from one side of the room to the other. "Trish," she admitted shortly. "And you are...Mason Ames, a friend of my mother's. That's what you said."

"Right."

She waited for a full explanation but none was forthcoming. He watched her, obviously knowing what she was after but unwilling to open himself to her just yet. Instead, he took a bite of the ice cream. "Want some?" he offered, gesturing with the spoon.

Trish could barely conceal her shudder. "No, thank you." She stood uncertainly. If only she had a better picture of just exactly what was going on here. She couldn't very well order him to leave, much as she wished she could.

She had to admit that if one were going to have an affair, this man looked as though central casting might have sent him over for the part. Rough but elegant, sensual but intelligent, he was perfect for anyone who wanted to step inside a fantasy life. She herself had never kissed a man who was so handsome, never been held by arms that looked that strong . . . but she banished those thoughts as soon as they came to her. Nevertheless, her heart was beating a little bit faster.

If her mother didn't come soon, she was going to have to leave. In the meantime, she glanced about the room wondering what to do next.

He watched her with interest, continuing to spoon the ice cream at the same time. "You here to check me out?" he asked suddenly.

"What?" She looked back at him and pulled her bag nervously to her chest. "What do you mean?"

That grin was back. The man actually had dimples. "Your sister was here earlier. And now you." He dug into the cardboard container and came up with a large chunk of brickle. "Are there any more of you coming by later?" The brickle popped into his mouth. "I'd like to think that I'd passed muster with the full set."

Trish watched his enjoyment of the ice cream, thinking some ice cream manufacturer ought to grab this guy for television commercials. Despite the tension between the two of them, he was enjoying his snack with open relish that seemed completely genuine. That sort of joy could be contagious. She took a deep breath to keep from letting down her shaky defenses. Shelley was absolutely right. This man was sexy. Their mother was lonely and confused and hurting . . . a prime target for this sort of sexy. Trish wished she could deny it, wished she could close her eyes and make it go away. She felt shaky, scared and hollow. This man was enough to make any woman think twice. How was she going to get him out of her mother's life?

"I don't know what you're talking about." Her voice was hardening now. She was more sure of her purpose.

He looked up at her again and grinned. "I don't mind. Check me out all you want. My life's an open book." His dark eyes sparkled with amusement. "Why don't you sit down?" he suggested. "You're making me nervous, standing over me like that."

Nervous! Resentment shot through her. He looked as relaxed as a cat on a hearth. She was the one who was uncertain here, and he knew it very well.

"I don't believe anything would make you nervous," she muttered. But she sank gingerly to the edge of the couch, sitting as far from him as she could get, thinking of things that were making *her* nervous, wondering vaguely if he would be offended if she asked him to button his shirt. Probably. She abandoned the idea and tried to think of a subtle way to pump him for information. Questions such as, "How long have you known my mother?" or "Have you been in San Diego long?" came to mind, but before she could stop herself, she blurted out, "Don't you have a job to go to?"

He put down the spoon and the empty ice cream container. "I'm sort of between jobs right now," he admitted, and his expression was suddenly guarded. "I left my last job and I'm looking forward to starting something new I've got lined up."

Something new? Shelley's description popped into her mind, along with the words they'd bandied about. Gigolo. Could he possibly mean...? She knew there were men who did this sort of thing for a living, latching on to older, wealthy women, giving them attention and a ready escort in return for a salary. Trish felt all the blood drain out of her face. It couldn't be. Could it? Was he really some kind of gigolo? Was her mother really so lonely she'd had to turn to this?

She closed her eyes for just a second, steadying herself, then looked back at him. Actually, she had to hand it to him. If that were his business, he was certainly attractive enough for it. His eyes had a knowing look, as though he knew what you were thinking just a half second before you knew it yourself. He looked strong, yet lazy, like a huge jungle animal, all leashed power behind sleepy eyes. There was something about that tousled hair that made you want to reach out and . . .

Stop it! she ordered herself silently, straightening her shoulders and steeling herself. This was ridiculous. She was here to figure out what to do about this man, not fall under his spell. Besides, at the same time she was studying him, it was perfectly evident he was doing the same to her, and she couldn't help but be curious as to what he saw.

She knew her copper-tipped hair was disheveled despite its neat, short cut, that her makeup had been worn away by now, revealing the freckles scattered across her nose, that her navy blue and white-trimmed, square-cut sailor dress was hopelessly gauche, that her soft leather navy flats looked much too sensible for one with his flamboyant tastes. If he had flamboyant tastes. But surely he must have.

She tried to read what he was thinking from the expression in his eyes, but all she saw there was slightly ironic humor. The man was laughing at her! How dare he!

"Do you have any idea when she'll be back?" she asked him stiffly.

He shook his head. "She left right after breakfast and she didn't tell me where she was going."

"I see." Right after breakfast! Trish's hands were clenched into fists, the nails biting flesh. A wave of nausea swept over her. How dare he state things so calmly! Her green eyes sent daggers. "I hope she fixed you something nutritious."

A half smile softened his face. "Actually, I fixed breakfast. A ham omelet. My specialty."

The man even cooked! "Who could ask for anything more," she muttered to herself in anguish.

"What was that?" He'd caught the thread of the emotion, but not the words.

"Nothing." She moved restlessly on the couch, at a loss as to what she was supposed to do, how she was supposed to react to this flagrant intruder in her family's life. "Nothing at all."

He was apparently catching every nuance now, fully aware of her unease and her confusion. And obviously resenting it somewhat.

"So what do *you* do?" he asked her, his dark eyes narrowing as though to prevent her from reading any more in his gaze. "Besides keeping tabs on your mother's life."

Yes, he knew what she was thinking, what she was upset about. Her chin rose and she met his gaze squarely. "I don't do any such thing!"

That eyebrow tilted upward again. "Oh, no? Then what exactly is it that you're doing here?"

His tone was light, almost bantering, as though he were teasing her. But she had the distinct impression that he was more serious than he pretended.

"Visiting," she said defensively. "What's wrong with a daughter visiting her mother?"

"Not a thing." He settled back into the corner of the couch and watched her, a wry smile wavering on his lips, though his eyes were darkening dangerously. "It's

touching, actually. I love these close family relationships. Heartwarming stuff.''

The edge of sarcasm was all too clear and it fired her
anger. "I'm so glad you approve," she retorted in kind.
"Your opinion is so important to me."

Her words were spoken in a tone meant to supply a
sting and he reacted instinctively, reaching out to take
hold of her shoulder with one large hand, while he said,
"I'm important to your mother. And that's all that
counts."

They stared at one another for a long moment, tension quivering in the air. She didn't pull away from his
hand. She wouldn't give him the satisfaction of knowing it threatened her. Instead she lifted her freckled nose
at a challenging angle and glared right back at him.

He seemed to be searching for something in her eyes,
and was half surprised when he found it. A bemused
smile began to soften his face, and suddenly he threw
back his shaggy head and laughed aloud, and his hand
gave her shoulder a caressing pat before it left her
altogether.

Watching him, the stream of sunlight from the open
window sparkling gold in his dark eyes, shooting gold
through his thick hair, washing gold across his tan skin,
she felt every instinct for self-preservation coming alert.
He was as smooth as aged cognac, as seductive as . . .

Seductive? Had she really thought that word? That
only made her glare all the harder.

"Whoa, wait a minute," he was saying softly, looking at her again. Smiling, he leaned back against the
pillows and put his arm behind her on the back of the
couch. "Let's start over, okay? I think we're heading
down a path whose only logical destination is nothing

short of nuclear war. What do you say we back up and try for another route?''

Seductive. Yes, that was the word, all right. Those sleepy bedroom eyes and that hard brown naked chest. . . . She hesitated and he leaned closer, hooking a finger in the cuff of her short sleeve.

"It's obvious that you don't like me being here in your mother's place," he said, studying her reaction. "But there's a logical explanation for my presence here."

She turned her shoulder so that the sleeve slipped from his grasp. His fingers brushed her arm as she turned and she had to steel herself to keep from looking at them.

"Is there a logical explanation?" she asked, and hope flared. What if there was? What if this could all be wished away! "I'd be interested in hearing it."

He opened his hand, stared at its emptiness, then pulled it back. His eyes were dark, clouded, and she couldn't tell if she'd offended him the way she'd jerked away from him. Perhaps she had. She wasn't sure why that made her a tiny bit sorry, but the fact that it did made her all the more wary of him.

"The truth is," he was saying, "your mother very kindly allowed me to come in and sleep on her couch when my apartment downstairs was flooded. Bad pipes. It'll be a few days before they can get the place back in living condition." He smiled disarmingly. "So you see, it's all very innocent."

She wished she could believe him. But so far, he hadn't been very convincing. "You met in the laundry room, I suppose." She hadn't meant it to be insulting, but somehow her tone didn't come out quite the way she'd intended, and he reacted.

He hesitated and something darkened his gaze for just a moment. "No...no, actually we met at Mammoth."

Well, there it was. The truth at last. All hope of a good explanation died with that admission. Why had they let their mother go on that ski trip to Mammoth all alone? They should have realized how vulnerable she would be to this sort of temptation. Ski instructors were notorious ladies' men. It was like a singles bar on ice up there.

"I see," she said, drawing in a shuddering breath. Her heart was breaking.

"No." His attempt at a smile was beginning to fray around the edges. "No, I don't think you do see. Your mother has been very kind to me. She's a very generous woman."

"Sure, she's always been generous, up to a point. Actually, she was never one to take in strays before."

"Strays?" He repeated it slowly. All humor drained from his eyes. She'd finally gone too far. "Is that what I look like to you?"

Trish swallowed hard, wishing she could recall the word. There didn't seem to be anything she could say to soften the implications he'd obviously derived from the term. She'd hurt his feelings. Well, hell! Let his feelings be hurt. He deserved it.

But when she looked into his dark eyes, she felt a rush of remorse. He was taking this far more seriously than she'd intended. She didn't want to insult him. All she wanted was for him to vanish, to disappear from her mother's life, so that things could get back to normal.

"Are you accusing me of seducing your mother?" he asked her bluntly.

Her mouth was dry and she couldn't answer.

"So what, Trish," he said softly, insinuatingly.
"What if I am. What if your mother and I are having a
mad, passionate affair right here. What possible business is it of yours?"

Her heart was beating very fast, and still no words
would come.

He rose from the couch and stood over her, his shirt
hanging free, his hands on his hips. "Your mother and
I are friends," he said, his voice quiet but barely con-
cealing his anger. "It's none of your business what that
includes. If you can't handle that, I'd say you're the one
who's got a problem. Don't try to lay it on me. Okay?"

Trish stared back at him. "My problem isn't really
with you at all," she said softly at last. She rose, carefully avoiding him, and started for the door. "Please tell
my mother that I stopped by." She turned and looked
back. The storm in his dark eyes was compelling. She
felt a strong urge to do something, say something, to
calm it. But what could she do? Shrugging helplessly,
she added, "I'll call her later."

And then she was out the door and hurrying toward
the stairs.

The man was real, the man was threatening. Her insides were in turmoil. It felt very much as though the
structure she'd built her life on was in danger of crumbling away. Mason Ames was a dream of a man. And
he was living with her mother!

She supposed she wasn't being very modern about all
this. People split up every day, each going on to new
partners. But "people" could do whatever they wanted,
her parents were different. She needed them together.
Their union formed the foundation of her life. If they
split up for good, her world would crumble, all control
gone. Why couldn't anyone else see that?

She had to make them see before it was too late.

Anger flashed through her. Where the hell was her father while all this was going on? He should be taking care of his woman. It was time she paid a visit to dear old Dad. Maybe she could shake him up to take some action.

Two

The sound of the heavy door closing reverberated through the apartment. Mason waited until the sound died down, then shook his head with a rueful grin. He shouldn't have done that. It had been a childish reaction. Junior high all the way. But he wasn't used to having women look at him with contempt in their eyes, and that was exactly what he'd seen in Trish's level green gaze. He hadn't liked it.

He turned off the television, then he picked up the empty ice cream carton and other debris and carried it all to the kitchen. The spoon and half-empty beer bottle went into the sink, the ice cream carton in the trash, and then he stared out the window at the blue-gray sea, his hands clenched over the rim of the sink.

Maybe she was right. What was he doing here anyway? Maybe he should have stayed in Mammoth where he belonged, gliding down the slopes, living for the snow and sunshine. Maybe this whole effort to turn over a new leaf was doomed before it began—a major waste of time.

He flexed his wide shoulders and sighed aloud. What the hell. He was here now. He might as well see this thing through. After all, he'd given his word to Laura Becker, and his word was the one thing he didn't play around with.

Turning back to the kitchen, he filled the kettle with water and set it on the stove. He turned on the flame, watching it leap up around the bottom of the pot. That's the way life should be, leaping up, eagerness, catching hold of experience with both hands. It hadn't been that way for him for some time now. The women, the good times—it all was beginning to blur.

"You're growing up, Mason," his sister Charity had told him just the other day when he'd attempted to articulate some of these feelings to her. "Finally!"

Growing up. He shook his head and glanced at his reflection against the black glass of the oven. Same old Mason as far as he could see. Same old Mason.

He heard the front door opening and his first thought was that Trish had come back. Adrenaline began to surge until he heard the sound of the newcomer's voice.

"Mason? You here?"

It was Laura. He felt a certain tension drain away, letting his shoulders relax. Laura Becker was a nice person. No adrenaline needed.

"Hi," he said, emerging from the kitchen to find Trish's mother dropping packages on the floor beside the couch. "Been shopping?"

"That I have." She looked up with a bright smile, an older version of her daughter's. "I got some things I knew you needed. Some handkerchiefs. A light wind-breaker.''

The tension came back with her words. There was a tenuous ambivalence to his situation here, something that needed to be resolved. She was a wealthy woman. And who was he? Nobody. A ski instructor. The implications were obvious, and he didn't like them.

''I can get my own things,'' he said gruffly.

She looked up quickly, her eyes registering surprise at his tone. ''Of course you can. But I was out. And I needed to shop.'' She smiled, trying to coax his good humor back. ''After all, I consider this therapy. Pure therapy. I needed to do something to lift my spirits and get myself in the mood for this operation of ours, and shopping did it.''

He hesitated, accurately reading her abundant good-will. Give her a break, he told himself scornfully. She's been nothing but great to you. She doesn't deserve this defensive attitude. He shrugged apologetically.

''Sorry, Laura. I didn't mean to snap at you. But I want to pay for my own things.'' He reached into his wallet and extracted a bill, placing it on the table. The kettle's whistle went off at a convenient moment. ''I'll get us some tea.''

He was back in a moment, carrying two earthenware mugs filled with the steaming herbal brew. He handed one to her, then joined her on the couch.

She took the mug, cupping it in her hands, and studied him for a long moment.

''Why the long face?'' she asked at last. ''You're the one who's usually trying to perk me up.''

He sank back into the corner of the couch and gave her a half grin. ''What is it? Are you turning telepathic on me? Reading my mind?''

She laughed. "I've been a mother for so many years, it just comes naturally."

He nodded, then frowned, toying with the handle on the mug. "You had a few visitors while you were out."

He could see her stiffen. "Oh?" she said carefully, putting down her mug on a coaster and using one index finger to wipe up a smudge on the table. "Who were they?"

"Your daughters dropped by. One at a time."

She turned back to face him, her expression relaxing into a smile. "And found you here." Her smile grew to a grin.

He reached for the family portrait she had displayed on the coffee table. "This one," he said, pointing to silver-haired Shelley, "arrived first, gaped at me, and ran for the door. Then this one," he went on, pointing to Trish's sunny face, "came storming over to check me out, obviously warned by her sister. She gave me the third degree, threw around a few insults, and stormed out again."

Laura Becker gasped in dismay. "What? That doesn't sound like Trish."

"Well . . ." His grin was a shade sheepish. "I might have provoked her a bit."

"I'll bet!" Laura laughed. "But didn't you tell them who you were, why you were here?"

"I tried." He shrugged. "I started to. But when it came right down to it, I wasn't sure how to explain it."

"You're right." She picked up her mug. "I haven't really thought that part through. What are we going to tell them?"

They both fell silent, neither of them coming up with anything particularly appropriate.

The truth would be the best thing to tell them, Mason thought to himself. Making up stories always ended in chaos. A half smile curled his lips as he remembered some of the scrapes he and his sister Charity had fallen into when they'd tried to pretend things were other than what they actually were. The truth was the only way to avoid that sort of thing. But he hesitated and finally decided not to prod Laura with that advice just yet. This was her show. She had a right to set it up in her own fashion.

Still, he decided on a cautionary note. "They've got the wrong idea, you know," he told Laura. "Especially Trish. And I'm afraid I got mad and let her walk out, still thinking what she was thinking."

Laura looked blank. "What do you mean? What was she thinking?"

To his total amazement, Mason felt color filling his cheeks. Blushing. He was blushing. Good God, what next? He shook his head again, smiling with self-deprecation. "She was thinking...that you and I...well, that we're here together...that we're more than just friends."

Laura stared at him. "My own daughters think something like that?"

Mason's eyebrows rose quizzically. "You can't see why they might make that mistake?"

Laura laughed. "Well, no, it's absurd. I mean, you're so...so...." She gestured incoherently toward him and made a face.

He looked down at himself, then back at her. "Thanks a lot, lady," he kidded her with a grin. "I guess I know where I stand."

"No!" She laughed. "Of course, you're a terribly attractive man. But you know that. All those little snow bunnies at Mammoth don't hang all over you for nothing." She sobered. "But I'm a bit beyond the snow bunny stage. I would have thought my daughters would have given me a bit more credit."

He cleared his throat. "Don't blame them," he said gruffly. "They're just concerned about you. They probably think I'm after your money or something." He shrugged.

Laura sighed. "And you're feeling uncomfortable about it." She shook her head. "You're doing me such a tremendous favor. Your coming down here to San Diego to help me is a godsend as far as I'm concerned. I was at my wit's end until I thought of bringing you in to help start up this business. You're going to be saving lives."

"Am I?" I hope so, he added silently. I hope it's going to do you a lot of good, because I'm not at all sure what good it's going to do me.

Laura was looking bemused. "So my daughters really were concerned?"

"Oh, yes. Very concerned."

"Maybe I'd better give Trish a call and let her know the truth." She sighed. "Though I know it's not going to be easy for her to accept it. She's always defended her father, and this is going to be perceived as an attack on him, I'm sure. Oh well, best get it over with."

Rising, she walked over to the telephone, tapping out the number on the buttons. "No answer." She shrugged, putting down the receiver. "I'll call her later." She turned back to Mason.

He was deep in thought, mulling over what she'd said. *Our Plan*. That was a euphemism. It had been Laura's plan right from the start. Mason stirred restlessly. He wasn't used to having someone else chart his life this way. He wasn't sure he'd be able to adjust.

But he didn't like the life he'd been living lately, either. He wasn't a kid any longer. He'd felt for some time he needed a change, but the right avenue hadn't come clear. And then Laura had come to him with her ideas, and they'd sounded like something worth looking into. So here he was. For now.

He stared at the family portrait on the coffee table again. The faces looked so happy. But then they always did in those things. His gaze concentrated on Trish's freckled face, then slid to the next figure in the shot. "How about him?" he asked, pointing to Laura's husband, Tam Becker. "Will he be coming around?"

Laura turned her face away so that he couldn't see the expression in her eyes. "Don't worry about him," she said softly. "He's got much more important things to do than to worry about my welfare."

Mason sat back against the couch again and stared at the mug in his hand. There was emotion in her voice, deep, abiding pain. The mother, the husband, two angry daughters. What the hell had he gotten himself into here?

Trish hurried through the lobby of the low building, waving at the receptionist and pushing her way through the wide double doors that led out onto the production floor. Saws and sanding machines screamed, but an occasional greeting was shouted above the noise and she waved at each workman. Most of them were people she'd known all her life. She went through another set of double doors into the research area, and there she found her father all alone, running his hands over the freshly wrapped coating on a brand-new surfboard.

"Hi, Daddy," she called as she approached.

He looked up and smiled at her, and despite the thinning blond hair, his grin was as boyish as it had been thirty years before when he'd formed his first surfboard with his own hands, the board that would launch one of the largest surfboard companies in the world. He'd been one of the first surfers on the California coast and those days were still a part of him. In spite of the cool March weather, he wore Bermuda shorts and a bright Hawaiian shirt, with thongs on his feet.

"Hi, sugar," he responded, turning to give her a hug and a loud smack on the cheek. "What's new?"

Too much to go into casually. She drew back and looked at him, deciding to get right to the point. "Daddy, don't you think it's time to make up with Mom?"

"Your mother?" He frowned as though that were a knot he didn't feel like untying at the moment. Turning away he went back to running his hand over the lemon-yellow board. "What about your mother?"

She steeled herself. She'd never been much of a pusher, but some things needed a bit of a shove, and this was one of them. "Don't you think this has gone on long enough?"

"Hmmmm?" He narrowed his eyes and leaned back to get another angle on his study of the paint job. "What's that?"

"She's never been gone for six months before."

His shoulders seemed to tighten, but he still examined the surface of the board for flaws. "Has it been that long?"

"You know it has!" She went around to the other side of the board to get back into his line of vision.

"What do you think of the patina on this resin?" he asked. "We've got a new supplier and I'm not sure about the luster—"

"Daddy! Listen to me! You're going to lose her!"

His head rose and he finally met her gaze. He stared at her for a long moment, his eyes unreadable. "Baby, I can't lose something I don't have," he said softly at last.

Something in the flatness of his dark eyes shocked her as much as his words did. What if it were already too late? She wasn't sure she could stand that. A hot, choked feeling filled her throat, but she forced herself to go on.

"Daddy, can't you talk over your differences? I . . . I have an idea. I'll invite her to dinner, but I won't tell her you're coming, too. . . ."

He turned away dismissively. "Forget it, sugar. Your mother and I have nothing to talk about."

She followed him, putting a hand on his arm. "Daddy, you've been married for over thirty years."

"And according to your mother, that's just about thirty years too long." Anger darkened his face. "She left me, Trish. I didn't leave her."

Trish shrugged helplessly. "But she's left before. . . ."

"Never for more than a few days." He turned and shoved his hands deep into his pockets. "She's never taken an apartment before."

Trish gestured into the air. "Maybe if you talked, you could find out why—"

"Damn it, Trish!" He slammed the table with the flat of his hand, making a resounding slap that hit her with almost physical force. His face was hard and dark, his eyes shining with anger. "She doesn't want me anymore. She told me so. I'm not going to go begging to get her back. It's over." He turned and began to stalk off toward his office. "I've got work to do," he grumbled, hurrying away.

She followed him and fired her last shot. "Daddy," she called out after him. "Mom's seeing someone else." Then she waited, holding her breath, to see if she'd made a very big mistake or not.

"Someone else?" His steps slowed. "You don't think I know about that?" He turned back, his brows drawn together. "Trish, this is something that's been coming for a long time. You're grown-up. Shelley is involved in her medical studies. You two don't need us to be together anymore. Just let it alone. We'll do what makes us happy. You don't have to worry about us."

Whirling, he slammed into his office, making it very clear he wouldn't welcome company.

Trish stood where she was, shaken to her roots. Tears rimmed her eyes and spilled down her cheeks. She felt empty and aching and she couldn't stand it. She had to do something. Anything, to keep from feeling so awful.

Get mad, she told herself fiercely. Anger was better than this nagging pain. She blinked away the tears. These were two very stubborn and pigheaded people she was dealing with here. It was obvious she was going to have to do more than talk. She was going to have to do some manipulating.

Three

———

Trish pulled her lime green convertible to a stop along the sand at Mission Bay and turned the engine off, watching the late afternoon sunlight dance across the water. There was a wild, gypsy twist to the wind that was kicking up along the shore. It tousled her hair and made her shiver uneasily.

Am I just being selfish, she wondered. Am I refusing to grow up? Is it my own insecurity? Do I need that family unit behind me because, so far, I haven't been able to build one of my own?

All of the above, she admitted. But also, she couldn't just dismiss it, that partnership that had sustained her for so many years, that loving nest that had nurtured two girls and molded them into women. It had worked so well for so long.

A part of her was crying, let it go! It's their business, not yours.

Another part of her was just crying. She wasn't sure why, but having her parents together and happy again was deeply important to her—fundamental. Now if only she could think of a way to bring that resolution about.

A sea gull called. The raucous sound of its voice filled her with a dreadful loneliness. She shivered again and reached for the key, turning the engine on. Gravel spit out as she raced away.

Her mother's apartment was nearby and she found herself pulling up before the building. Something told her she would have no more luck getting through to her mother than she'd had with her father, but it was worth a last ditch effort. Striding briskly into the courtyard, the first thing she saw was Mason Ames doing laps in the apartment pool.

She hesitated behind a huge bird of paradise in full bloom. She didn't relish another run-in with the man. But his head was down and he was swimming energetically back and forth. He hadn't seen her. Maybe it would be possible to sneak by him. The pool was long and serpentine, but if she just walked quickly, head high, eyes on the stairs ahead....

She almost made it. Just as she neared the far end of the pool she heard a great surge in the water, and then there he was, standing before her, beads of water flying everywhere—including all over her.

"Hello, Trish," he said calmly. "You came back."

She backed away, shaking drops of water from her hair and glaring at him. "But not for a swim," she protested. "And not to see you."

"Of course not. I know you came to see your mother. But I wanted to talk to you first."

She backed away another foot or two. The man was practically naked. Silver streams of water ran over his tanned flesh, making him look slick and smooth. His swimsuit was a tiny strip of electric blue material that didn't so much hide as accentuate. His thighs were thick and strong and covered with dark hair. His wet shoulders seemed wider than ever. The entire effect was like some exotic dream of a lover one might conjure up on a lazy summer afternoon. But at the same time he was much, much too real.

She winced, as though protecting herself from too bright a light. If she let him, he could easily weaken her defenses. "Talk fast," she said breathlessly, trying to still her pounding heart. "I'm in a hurry."

His eyebrows rose and his hands went to his hips. "Is it just me?" he asked her. "Or are you this rude to all the men you know?"

She flushed, shocked. No one had accused her of being rude since she was six years old and refused to kiss Aunt Lulu goodbye. But she knew he was absolutely right. She was being unforgivably rude.

Turning away she stared at the still water of the pool. "I'm sorry if you think I'm rude to you," she said, trying hard to control her voice. "I guess I tend to forget my manners when I'm upset."

She glanced up and for just a moment she thought his dark eyes actually showed concern. "What have I done to upset you?" he asked quietly.

What a question! It worked on every level, from the purely sensual, to the moral, to the intellectual. Any way you sliced it, he was an upsetting man.

"That's not precisely the point," she answered evasively. She looked at him, tried to think of how to tell him just what the point was, and failed, distracted once again by his well-built body. "Do you ever appear any-where fully dressed?" she asked in exasperation.

His grin started at his eyes and grew from there. "Not if I can help it. I'm a nature freak. How about you?" But he reached for a towel, dabbing with it at his chest.

She shook her head, but the grin was having its effect. "I think nature is best tamed," she claimed. "Like you ought to be." Her face softened.

Mason hesitated, hearing the emotion in her voice and reacting viscerally. For some crazy reason, she touched him. He looked at her with her unhappy face and her anguished eyes and he wanted to pick her up and hold her and tell her everything was going to be all right. But she wouldn't like that. That much was obvious. So he said instead, "Why can't we be friends?"

"Friends?" She seemed confused by the concept.

"Friends. You know, people who say 'Hello' and 'How are you?' and 'Nice weather,' and 'Hey, do you want to go with me to see a movie sometime?' instead of 'Make it fast, I'm in a hurry.'"

She was still stunned by the thought. "We...we can't be friends. We're on opposite sides."

He nodded slowly. "You see, that's what I don't really understand. Opposite sides of what? What's the war here?"

He waited for a moment but she didn't answer. "Okay, tell me this. What can I do to make you stop hating me?"

Hating. The word shocked her. She didn't hate him. How could he think that? She looked into his eyes and slowly shook her head. "I don't hate you," she said softly. "Don't you understand? I just don't want my mother hurt...."

"Trish." He dropped the towel and put his hands on her shoulders, staring down into her green eyes, searching them for something. "Come with me," he said abruptly. "I've got to talk to you."

"But..." She looked back at the apartment as he took her by the hand and led her into a secluded gazebo at the corner of the courtyard. Honeysuckle climbed about the structure in thick profusion, cutting off visual access and filling the air with perfume.

"Sit." He sat beside her on the small white wicker love seat. Turning toward her he took her hand, holding it palm up and placing his other hand over it. His face was earnest. "Now listen to me."

How was she going to listen when she was so busy trying to keep her senses from spinning out of control? Where had this man come from, some other planet? Her heart was pounding, her head reeling. He was so close, she could feel him, like a laser imprint of heat. His large, strong hands held hers captive, warming her all over. She couldn't speak. She could hardly think.

"Your mother and I are not lovers," he said slowly, distinctly, gazing intently into her eyes. When she didn't respond, he reached out with one hand and drew an invisible line across her cheek with one index finger. "Are you listening? Have you got that? We are not lovers. Period."

Her green gaze was locked with his dark one. Her cheek tingled where he'd touched it. She nodded slowly. "Got it," she whispered. And suddenly she knew he was telling the truth. She couldn't possibly feel this way—this incredible, breath-stopping way—about a man who was having an affair with her mother.

"Good," he said, and sighed with relief. "Okay, here's the story. I've known your mother for a couple of years. She's been coming up to Mammoth pretty regularly. And she's become friendly with my sister, Charity, who has a restaurant up there. The two of them cooked up this scheme to have me come down here with your mother and help her . . . with a project she's got going."

"A project?"

He hesitated. This wasn't his story to tell. "She wants me to help someone run his business. In effect, she's helping me get a job."

"Oh."

"And since I was tired of what I was doing, I said okay. Why not give it a try?" He looked at her closely, wondering if she understood. She looked shell-shocked.

"I got myself an apartment in this building, and then my pipes burst and I needed emergency shelter. Your mother took me in. End of story. Got it?"

Trish nodded. "Got it," she whispered again. She was relieved. She should have known it all along. It had just been a momentary lapse, a quick panic that grew from the seed Shelley had planted. When she'd seen how gorgeous he was. . . . She knew better now. The idea seemed absurd. He was so very. . .

Her gaze dropped to his mouth and she wondered how he kissed and suddenly she would have given almost anything to find out. She swayed toward him, lost in a wave of sensory longing that she couldn't begin to understand.

Mason stared at her. He wasn't sure if she'd taken in the things he'd said. She had such a dreamy look on her pretty, freckled face. It would have been the most natural thing in the world for him to reach out and draw her into an embrace, to taste that sweet-looking mouth. He was an old hand at seduction, and she was looking definitely seducible. Old habits die hard and attractive women had always been his downfall.

His hands started to move of their own accord, but he clenched them into fists and swore silently to himself. No, dammit! This was just what he had to avoid. If this new life he was starting was going to mean anything at all, he had to teach himself to stop doing things just because they were easy and tempting to do. It was time to develop a little restraint, a little character.

Besides, this woman before him was not at all his usual type. She scared him a little. He sensed something different about her. He was very much afraid that he could touch her, kiss her, and find himself unable to turn around and walk away. He'd never given up control before. Could he handle it? He wasn't sure. He braced himself to hold back his natural responses, even though she was making herself so temptingly available right now.

"So you do understand," he mumbled, avoiding her eyes. "Great. Okay."

Trish stared at him and reached to steady herself on the back of the love seat. She felt like she was coming down from a roller coaster ride, her balance still not certain. What was going on here? What had she been doing?

He was embarrassed, uncomfortable, looking out across the courtyard and scrunching up in the corner of the seat, getting as far away from her as possible. She blinked hard, clearing her mind. Wait a minute. What had she done here?

Her mind was still just coming out of its fog, but she knew one thing. She'd been in a swoon, overcome by Mason's charms. And he'd been very well aware of it. And had chosen to do nothing about it.

She jumped up from the love seat, her face stained with an agonized red. "Of course, I understand perfectly well," she said, looking down at her hands, out at the pool, anywhere but at him. "If you'd told me this in the first place, you could have saved us both the hassle."

"Trish . . ." He stood and took a step after her.

She backed away very quickly. "See you around, Mr. Mason Ames," she said as breezily as she could muster. She met his gaze for a moment, felt the pull of his strong personality, and looked away again as fast as she could. And then she was off, hurrying toward the stairs, praying he wouldn't follow her.

She'd never been so embarrassed before in her life. How could she have done that, losing all control that way, letting her hormones spin her into a romantic mist that clouded her brain? She'd always been the sensible one, the one who looked before she leaped. How could she have made such a fool out of herself?

Her hand was shaking as she knocked on the door of her mother's apartment and she took a deep breath to steady herself.

"Hi," she said brightly when her mother opened the door, hoping she wouldn't notice anything amiss.

Laura's face broke into a wide smile and she gave her oldest daughter a hug and a quick kiss on the cheek. "Trish, darling! Hi, there. Come on in."

She drew her daughter into the room, then turned and displayed the open back of her silk dress. "Just in time, too. I need help. I'm really in a hurry. Can you zip me, please? Thanks, dear."

She whirled, the brightly colored skirt of her dress whipping around her shapely legs, and Trish stared at her as if she were seeing her for the first time.

She really was beautiful. Her eyes were alight with excitement. She looked full of life and full of fun. Laura Becker was an engaging, attractively packaged bundle of femininity and any man with any life left in him couldn't help but like what he saw. Any man at all.

Trish felt cold. Where did that leave her father?

Laura swept through the room, searching for her purse. "I hear you've met Mason. Did you see him down at the pool?" she asked happily.

"Yes," Trish said slowly. "I . . . I saw him."

"Isn't he a doll?"

"I . . . well, he's certainly . . ."

Laura didn't seem to notice her hesitation. "Listen, how do I look?" She posed before her daughter. "I'm going over to see Bert."

Trish frowned, puzzled. "Dad's old partner?" Bert and Tam had been surfing buddies. Together they'd formed Becker's Boards when they were in their twenties. Tam had always been the best surfer, the one who intuitively knew just what to do to a board to make it better. Bert had handled most of the business end of the partnership. Their friendship and business arrangement had lasted through the years, until about eighteen months before when Bert had suffered a heart attack. He'd retired soon after, leaving the company to Tam. Bert was unmarried, a playboy of the old school, and Laura had never fully approved of him. "What are you going to see him for?"

Laura shrugged, glanced at her daughter and then away. "I've got some things I want to discuss with him." She started toward the door. "I'm sorry I have to run out just now, when you've finally come to see me. But I made the appointment and I've got to keep it." She laughed. "You know Bert. If I'm not there on time, he'll be off riding around in that sports car of his with some blond floozy before you know it.''

She said the words with affection. What had happened to her usual disapproval? Trish bit her lip worriedly. Had her mother gained some new perspective on life? If so, she didn't think she was going to like it.

"Are you planning to go to the Regatta on Saturday?" Trish asked hopefully.

"Of course. We always go to that, don't we?" She patted a bit of hair into place. "I'm bringing Mason along, to meet people. He needs to get into the swing of things around here." She whirled. "Well, I must be off." She threw Trish a wide smile. "You be a sweetheart and take care of Mason for me while I'm gone, won't you? Entertain him or something. I won't be long."

Trish stiffened. "I'm sorry, Mother, but I have things I have to do," she said.

"Oh. That's a shame. Well, he's a pretty resourceful guy. I guess he'll be able to take care of himself."

"I'm sure of it."

Laura laughed, obviously oblivious to the edge of irony in Trish's tone. "Come on and walk out with me, then. We'll have a short chat on the way to the car."

Trish followed her mother, but she didn't feel much like chatting. Her mind was full of unwelcome thoughts. It looked very much as though her mother were embarking on a new life. Trish hated every piece of evidence that she saw. But did she really have any right to try to stop her?

"See you later!" Laura called as she drove off.

Trish stood on the sidewalk and watched her disappear around the corner. She hadn't said any of the things she'd meant to. She hadn't even asked her mother how things stood. Maybe that was because she was afraid to hear the answer.

She dug her keys out of her purse, then hesitated, holding them so tightly in her palm, the sharp edges cut into her skin.

"Trish."

She knew it was Mason without turning to look, but she turned to look anyway. He'd found a thick, silver terry cloth robe, but it was very short and his muscular legs were still bare. It wasn't fair that he was so attractive. It wasn't fair that she had suddenly become so susceptible to that kind of attractive.

"Trish, I think we should talk."

She was already shaking her head, already backing away. She'd made enough of a fool of herself for one day. "Sorry," she said breathlessly, turning to her car. "I'm in a hurry." She pulled open the door and dropped onto the seat, looking back at where he stood at the entrance to the courtyard. "I...uh..." She shrugged helplessly. Oh, the hell with it! "Goodbye." And she was off, leaving him standing behind watching her go.

"Why me?"

Trish and Shelley were in her bedroom trying on dresses from Shelley's closet. Trish was holding up a Hawaiian print sundress to her chest and gazing critically in the full-length mirror.

"Why am I elected?" Dropping the dress on a chair, she turned and looked at Shelley beseechingly. "Why do I have to be the one to keep Mason Ames captive at the Regatta?"

"Listen, darling," Shelley drawled, flopping down on the bed in a halter-top minidress that showed off long brown legs. "This is your idea. Your crusade. So you get to do the dirty work."

"But you're so much better with men like that. You've had so much more experience."

Shelley fixed her with a suspicious glare and adjusted her huge, lilac-tinted glasses, reminding Trish of a European count with a monocle. "And just exactly what is that supposed to mean?" she demanded.

"Oh, Shelley, you know what I mean. You know how to handle his type. A ladies' man." She sank down on the bed beside her sister and looked her over with a mixture of affection and exasperation. Shelley had always been the "brain" of the family, her nose constantly in a book. And yet every time she looked up myopically, there was some handsome man looking back, smiling a hopeful invitation to something fun. Shelley always seemed to sigh with resignation and go out with her mind only half on her date. And men flocked to her anyway—though Shelley hardly seemed to notice. She was heavily involved in her medical studies right now. A born student, she still attracted playboys.

In marked contrast, Trish often thought, to the sort of male that seemed to naturally gravitate toward her. "The men I go out with are more likely to wear desert boots than Italian leather shoes," she reminded her little sister now. "They carry slide rules and fall asleep in the middle of candlelight dinners. They take the bus because it's cheaper and show up with candy that they proceed to eat themselves."

"If your guys are still carrying slide rules, you really are in trouble" was Shelley's only comment.

"Well, calculators then. Nerds on wheels. That's all I ever get."

Shelley choked back her laughter, hearing the desperation in Trish's voice. "They're not that bad," she noted dryly. "But I do see your point." She thought for a moment, then shook her head, her long blond hair flying about her shoulders. "No, I won't do it. You're the one who wants to push Mom back into Dad's arms, not me. I say, leave them alone and let nature take its course."

"But you will help me."

Shelley shrugged. "Oh, all right. I'll waylay Mom at the Regatta. Sure. But I won't flirt with Mason. You'll have to do that."

The Regatta was an annual event staged at the Bay Club. The wealthy Bournane family put it on. The yacht race itself covered the span from Verde Point to the marina at the Bay Club. An elegant banquet was laid out at the finish, and everyone who was anyone on the lower South Coast came to celebrate. The Beckers had attended every year since Tam's surfboards had first taken off in the marketplace. If you were involved in water sports in the area, it was something you just didn't miss.

"I can't do it," Trish murmured, but Shelley paid no attention.

"I'll take charge of Mom the moment she arrives. You'll steer Mason off in some other direction. I, working with finesse and casual subtlety, will lead Mom to where Dad is and throw them together."

Trish sighed and looked wistful. "They'll see each other from across the way. The roses will be in full bloom, framing their views. Memories will surge in each of them. Longings. Regrets." She sighed again. "It better work."

Shelley yawned.

"In the meantime," Trish reminded herself in trepidation. "*I'm* stuck with Mason Ames."

Shelley rolled onto her back, head down off the bed, and added, "Oh, quit complaining. You have the easiest part. Mason Ames is a hunk. You know how gorgeous he is. Enjoy him."

Trish gave her an outraged glare. "You don't enjoy a man like a . . . like a piece of cake."

"Why not? I always do."

They were silent for a long moment mulling that over. A picture of Mason's handsome face floated into Trish's mind, demanding attention. What was he going to make of all this? It was hard to tell. Every time she'd been near him her emotional antennae had been messed up by her physical reactions to him. No man had a right to be that appealing. Every time she thought of how she'd fallen under his spell the day before, she got red all over again. She just wasn't used to men like that. She'd be stronger the next time.

She shivered. The next time was coming right up, all too soon. She moaned softly and closed her eyes. Keep Mason occupied, distracted, and out of her mother's hair so that her mother and father could have a chance to make up in peace—those were her marching orders. Her heart beat very fast, but she told herself she would do it. Somehow.

Mason took a long look at himself in the full length mirror. He didn't often dress up so formally. The jacket was cut just right, though, and he'd never worn a whiter shirt. Laura had picked well.

"Wow, aren't you pretty?" Laura laughed over his shoulder. "I didn't realize there was such a handsome gentleman underneath all that suntan lotion."

He looked quickly into her eyes and tried to smile. He knew she was just kidding, but something in her words stung. Funny. He'd been getting awfully sensitive about his playboy image lately. There'd been a time when he'd been proud of it. But now, when he looked in the mirror at his maturing features, the image didn't seem to fit. There was something missing. His eyes seemed to be asking: is that all there is? And waiting for his heart to answer.

But he managed to turn and smile at her. "Am I going to be presentable for all your friends?"

"Oh, sure." She fluffed her hair and reached for a lipstick. "But you'd be presentable in shorts for my friends. They aren't the ones you're putting on the dog for." She slashed some color on her lips. "It's Bert that we want to impress today. I want you to meet him and I want you to make him sit up and take notice. Okay?"

He saluted. "I'll do my best, boss."

"I'm not your boss." She grinned at him. "Not yet, anyway."

He smiled and turned back to the mirror, straightening his tie. "Who else is going to be there?" he asked casually. "Your family?"

"You mean my daughters?" She pulled a shawl out of the closet and drew it around her shoulders. "They wouldn't miss it for the world." She turned to look at herself in the mirror. "And neither would my... husband, Tam. I suppose you'll have to meet him, too. But the girls will make sure you're entertained."

Mason hesitated and then said lightly, "I suppose they'll arrive with their respective husbands, fiancés, boyfriends, et cetera?" His tone was careless but he watched her eyes closely as she answered.

Laura paused and frowned. "No. Actually, neither of my girls has ever married." She was silent for a moment. "Strange, isn't it?" she said softly at last. "They grew up in a relatively happy home." She shook herself. "Tam and I had our problems through the years, but when we were together..." She sighed and her eyes grew slightly misty. "When we were together, we felt we had it all. You'd think they would have wanted to recreate that in their own lives, wouldn't you? And yet neither of them seems to want to take the step." She shook her head and said softly, "Maybe they didn't understand how very good the good times were."

Mason watched her, not really sure why this should make her unhappy. "I wouldn't worry about it," he said. "They seem like well adjusted young women. Look at Trish—"

"Trish!" She threw up her hands. "She's the worst of the lot. Ever since she bought herself that business, Paper Roses, she's become just like her father. Work, work, work. That's all she cares about." She glanced at her watch. "We're late! Come on. Bert is always late himself, but just in case, we'd better get going."

He went to the door and waited while she bustled about, searching for her bag, her keys, her handkerchief, chattering the whole time. He hardly heard her. His mind was on her copper-headed daughter. Another encounter with Trish was coming up. It was hard to ignore the fact that the prospect gave him a decided lift. He looked forward to seeing those emerald green eyes again—sparks and all.

Four

___

Saturday had dawned bright and warm. The Bay Club was decorated with Chinese paper lanterns and bushels of flowers. An orchestra played in the ballroom. A rock band played in the back lawn gazebo. Leis of vanda orchids, flown in from Hawaii, were being handed out to every woman present. The sea breeze tasted like champagne. It was a perfect day, a perfect setting. What could go wrong on a day like this?

"Just about anything," Trish murmured to herself cynically. She was outside the Bay Clubhouse, lurking in the bushes and feeling like a forest gnome. The plan had *sounded* good.

"We'll stay in among those camellia bushes by the entryway," she'd told Shelley. "Then we can pounce on Mason and Mom the moment they drive up."

But Mason and her mother had yet to make an appearance. One could only pretend fascination with camellias for so long, and then one began to look a bit loony hanging about, pawing flowers for hours on end. Shelley had already given up in disgust, and Trish was having doubts of her own.

Their father had already arrived right on time in his shiny white sports car. Shelley and Trish had stayed in the bushes, keeping out of sight, and he'd gone on in. But now Shelley was out on the walk beside the driveway, surrounded by admiring men as usual.

She can't help it, Trish always told herself, mostly as consolation. It's in the pheromones or something. She gives off some sort of a subliminal vibration that men can't resist. They're drawn to her, and they don't even know why. Trish had to admit she'd had twinges of envy now and then.

Not that she'd ever been a wallflower herself, exactly. But the men who were interested in her never seemed to be just what she was interested in herself. She'd always thought that maybe if she had the vast numbers to select from that Shelley had, she'd find that perfect man.

Then again, it didn't seem to have done Shelley much good. She still dated a different man every night. "There's safety in numbers," she would say carelessly when anyone questioned her about it. "Endless variety keeps me from making mistakes." The perfect man was evidently elusive.

The perfect man—as if there really were such a thing. Trish sighed and watched one car after another drive up. The doorman in white livery stepped smartly about each car, helping out the ladies and allowing the attendants to park the cars in the nearby lot. Every now and then Trish spotted someone she knew, and at moments like that she was glad to be hiding in the greenery. At least she didn't have to try to explain why she was hanging around outside and wouldn't go into the banquet room.

"Hi, Trish," a voice said suddenly from the walkway.

Trish looked up quickly. Howie Servig smiled at her, his hazel eyes bright with appreciation, his silver-blond hair slicked down on his round head, the quintessential surfer, all grown-up.

"Oh. Hi, Howie." She smiled back, then licked her lips nervously. Howie had been her number one suitor since seventh grade. The more she tried to turn him gently away, the more stubbornly he clung. He'd gone away to college, then for a four year stint as an officer in the navy, and each time she'd breathed a sigh of relief, thinking this time, for certain, he would find someone else to fixate on. But no. He came back with that same smile, that same light of love in his eyes. Like a huge cocker spaniel, he would never desert her.

"You look great," he said, examining her rainbow pastel sundress, its skirt cut like tattered silk rags, its bodice low and revealing, its back showing a lot of bare skin with crisscrossing straps. It was Shelley's, actually, and a lot more daring than the things Trish usually wore. "Body language," Shelley had told her. "Learn it. Use it. Display it in a dress that knows the idiom." Trish felt slightly awkward dressing in something that looked like it might have been picked up in a lingerie shop, but she knew she did look good.

"You really look great," Howie repeated. "As always."

"Thanks. So do you." She smiled again and nodded, hoping he would take the hint and go on into the building.

But no. He reached out to part some branches so that he could get a better look at her. "Want some company?" he asked, his voice childishly hopeful.

Resisting the urge to shoo him away, she tried to smile again. "No, thanks just the same."

Ignoring her answer he took a step forward and glanced around curiously. "What is it?" he asked. "Are you meeting someone in here?"

She started to make a quick denial when it came to her that this might be just the chance she'd been searching for all these long years. For once she actually was meeting someone. It wouldn't be a lie at all.

"Why...uh...as a matter of fact, yes, Howie," she told him. "That's exactly what I'm doing. Meeting someone." Her smile quivered at the corners. "Secretly," she added for emphasis.

"Oh, I see." Howie never got angry, never got jealous. It was as though he thought if he just waited long enough, she'd get over her silliness and admit she loved him, too. "Who is he?"

"Uh...you don't know him."

"Does this mean...." He came in closer and looked down at her sadly. "Does this mean it's all over between you and me?"

Trish swallowed and looked around for help. There was nothing between them, and never had been, except for some figment of Howie's fertile imagination. But maybe he would feel better if there were a definite end to it. Just maybe that would set the poor man free.

"I guess it means exactly that, Howie," she said shakily. "It's been...interesting."

He took her hand and gazed at her soulfully. "He must be a wonderful man, Trish, if you've finally given your heart away."

She frowned. "Well, Howie, I haven't exactly..."

He put up a hand to stop her. "You don't have to apologize to me. I want what's best for you. And if this man is what you want, he's what I want, too."

She didn't know how to answer that, but maybe it didn't matter. At least he was backing away.

"Do you want me to stand guard or anything?" he asked helpfully.

"No. No, Howie, I don't think that will be necessary. But thanks for asking."

"Oh. Okay, then. I guess I'll go on in."

"Yes, you go on in. I'll see you in there in just a little while." She waved. He waved. And finally he was gone.

Diverted by Howie she hadn't noticed that her mother and Mason had arrived until she heard her mother's voice greeting Shelley. Quickly she slipped out from the camellias. Shelley threw her a significant look, drawing Laura with her toward the path to the rose garden. Trish knew Shelley would tell her mother not to worry about Mason, that Trish would entertain him until Laura was free again. She looked at the man as he got out from behind the wheel and took a deep breath. At least he was dressed for once.

She hated this—especially after the way she'd lost her head over him the other day. Once she put this little plan into motion, he would really think she'd flipped over him. Knowing that made her moan and bite her lip. But there was no other option that she could see. She had to do it for the sake of her parents' marriage.

"Here goes," she whispered to herself, stepping quickly to his side.

"Hi there." She put on her brightest smile as she approached him. Did she look coquettish? Or just plain demented? There was no way to tell. His reactions would have to be her guide.

He turned and looked at her in surprise. "Hi," he replied but it was almost a question, and there was nothing but question in his eyes.

He was dressed in a light suit, his white shirt starched to perfection, his rich, dark hair combed back carefully. Altogether, he was stunningly elegant looking. Her smile wavered a bit. Clothes didn't help. He was still a slice of pure erotic enticement in her book. But she couldn't let that throw her.

"I want to talk to you," she told him softly, slipping her hand under his arm and looking up at him with what she hoped was a seductive glance from under her eyelashes. "Will you come with me to a place where we can be alone?"

"Alone?" His eyes said, Is this a trick? but he nodded warily. "Sure," he said aloud. "But Laura..."

They both looked around. Laura and Shelley were disappearing around a far corner. Mason frowned. Trish moved in closer.

"Shelley's been waiting to talk to Mom. And I..." She batted her eyes and simpered, feeling sick but driven, "have been waiting to talk to you."

He looked at her for a long moment, his gaze skimming over her face, her shoulders, her body, tracing the low neckline, the soft swell of her breasts. She resisted the urge to put her hands up to cover all that bare skin. She could hardly stand this!

There'd been times in her young life when she'd mulled over trying for a more alluring role. It had seemed that it might be fun to play the seductive woman once in a while. Now she knew how wrong she'd been. She felt like a bit player in a Mae West movie. *Get me out of this!* she pleaded silently, glancing toward the building. Just a few more moments and she'd have him up on the captain's walk where she planned to keep him away from everyone else. Then she could drop this pretense and go back to being Trish Becker again.

But for now she was Miss Femme Fatale. Leaning close she clung to his arm. "Come on," she whispered provocatively.

Mason looked down at her. At first his gaze was quizzical, but as he took in her melting look and the picture she made in her skimpy dress, the look changed for one flashing second, opening up and revealing exactly what he was thinking. For the first time in her life Trish gazed straight into a look of pure, undiluted male hunger.

Her head snapped back and she gasped. But he didn't seem to notice. His arm tightened on her hand, tucking it in against his body. "Sure," he said huskily. "Let's go."

Her heart was thumping like crazy. They walked toward the entrance, arm in arm, but had to wait at the doorway. Six or seven other couples were lined up, taking their time going into the banquet room. She could feel Mason studying her but she didn't look up. She'd done her seductive number and she wasn't prepared for an encore just yet. She only wished the line would hurry up so she could get him up those stairs.

And then what? She shivered suddenly.

"Cold?" Before she could stop him he'd shrugged out of his suit coat and draped it around her shoulders and it was too late to tell him she wasn't cold at all, just nervous.

"You ought to put this back on," she warned him. "They might not let you in without a jacket on."

He only grinned again. "Pretty silly, isn't it? They won't let me in without a jacket, and yet they'll let you in without much more than a G-string and tassles."

Indignation swept through her, but at the same time she flushed with embarrassment. Glancing down at her filmy dress, she protested, "I didn't think it was that bad."

"Not bad. Good." His gaze began a lazy trip up and down the length of it. "Very, very good."

Trish struggled, but it was no use. She tried to bring back the seductive pose. She tried to smile and cock her head to the side and flutter her eyelashes. But it wouldn't work. She'd done all the posing she could possibly do in one day. In spite of all her efforts the real Trish sputtered forth.

"Listen, Mason Ames," she said evenly through gritted teeth. "This dress is a Galvaton original. There's nothing G-stringy about it."

"Isn't there?" He continued his caressing examination of her. "No, I guess you're right. It's more like... Have you ever heard of that stripper back in the thirties who danced with veils....?"

She punched him in the shoulder, then purposely let the coat drop. He caught it just before it hit the ground. At the same time he took hold of her arm, pulling her around to face him.

"Okay, Trish," he said softly. "Fun's over. Do you want to tell me what's going on here? What exactly you are playacting at?"

"I'm not...."

"You are."

Trish swallowed hard and pulled away from him, starting to back away, shaking her head, leaving the line behind. The femme fatale was so far gone now she knew she would never get it back.

"Trish!" He covered the distance between them and stood in the way of her retreat. "Let's have it. The truth."

"I don't know what you're talking about. I was just trying to be friendly."

"No." He dismissed her answer out of hand. "The role of seductress doesn't suit you at all. You don't have the knack for it." He glanced down at her dress again. "Though I must say, you do have the body."

She flushed, sputtering.

His hand went to her chin, tilting her sparking green eyes up toward his face. "What is it, Trish?" he asked, his dark gaze full of humor, but knowing. "Why can't you be straight with me?"

She still didn't answer. What would he do if she told him the truth, that she was trying to keep him away from her mother so her father could have a chance? Would he be insulted? Angry? She couldn't tell.

His fingers tightened. "It must be something pretty important," he said softly, his eyes darkening, filling with more than humor, more than question. "Coming on to me like that could have dangerous repercussions. Don't you know when you're playing with fire?"

She couldn't seem to catch her breath. With him so close, touching her, she had an overwhelming sense of his strength and of her own lack of it. She tried to think of something to say, some way to cover for what she'd been doing, but her mind seemed to be spinning in a fog of confusion.

Through the mist, she heard her name being called. Looking up, slightly dazed, she saw Howie coming their way, his wide face jovial, his hand stretched out.

"Is this him, then? The lucky man?"

"What?" She looked at him blankly, then remembered. "Oh, yes, I guess.... No! No!"

But it was too late. Howie stuck out his hand and Mason took it rather gingerly. "How do you do," Howie said solemnly. "Howie Servig, here."

"This...this is Mason Ames," Trish admitted reluctantly.

"Mason Ames. I'll remember that name." Howie beamed. "I just want to congratulate you. You're getting a fine woman. I hope you know that."

Mason's eyes clouded over. He looked from Howie to Trish's evasive gaze and back again. His expression was incredulous.

"Thank you," he said, though it sounded almost like a question.

"I know she'll make you happy. She's a lovely, lovely woman."

"Oh, yes." Mason's smile was slow and wondering. "I can see that. And you're right." His glance swept over her. "I'm sure she'll make me very happy."

Trish didn't like the sound of his voice. She smiled nervously at Howie and wished the earth would swallow him up. "Thank you, Howie," she said as he bent to kiss her cheek.

"No, Trish," he said solemnly. "Thank you for all the years of joy. They're over now." He sighed heavily. "But I guess the best man has won."

Turning, he walked sadly away. Mason grabbed Trish's arm and pulled her close again. "What the hell was that?" he muttered.

She tried to pull out of his grasp but it was no use. "Never mind," she whispered back. "We've got to get back in line or we'll never get in to the party."

They started back but before they reached the line someone else was calling to Trish.

Jerry Bates was the club photographer, and now he was rushing forward, camera in hand and hailing them, his thin face animated, his thin arms flailing.

"Ah, Miss Becker, we've heard about the forth-coming nuptials." He beamed at them both, then whipped out his tripod in the manner of one who'd done exactly that a thousand times before. "So pleased, indeed, so pleased." Waving for them to stand closer, he went on as though they'd ordered this session them-selves. "We'd love to get a picture of the two of you for our yearly photo collage. Do you mind? So nice of you!" He set his camera. "Now if you'd just kiss the bride-to-be, sir..."

Mason looked down at Trish, laughter in his eyes. "I didn't know we were getting married," he said.

She tried to smile. "I...I can explain every-thing..."

"Later," he agreed. "Right now I've got to kiss you."

"No, oh no!" She shook her head vehemently. "No, you don't have to do that."

He glanced at the beaming photographer, then looked back at Trish. "Yes." He reached for her. "I do." And from the gleam in his eye she knew he was going to do it.

"Nooooo," she protested, trying to back away. But he'd already swept her up into his arms.

"They want to see us kiss, darling," he said firmly. "I think we owe it to them. Don't you?"

"No!" She shook her head again but it was no use. His face was close, his breath hot and ticklish against her lips, and then his mouth was on hers and she might as well have fallen down a rabbit hole.

Something magic happened. She'd expected to be thrilled by his kiss. In fact, in her secret heart of hearts, she'd actually wondered what it would be like to kiss Mason. Stirring, she was sure. Exciting. But she'd never expected this.

It was the kiss on the banks of the Seine, the kiss in Rick's café, the kiss in the South American jungle as the arrows zing through the air. It was the old-fashioned movie kiss that she'd dreamed of all her life and never had before. Here, in front of all these people, it happened.

His arms around her were hard and steady, supporting her as she'd never been supported before. His breath was sweet and warm, his face slightly rough, but his touch was tender, and his mouth... his mouth was a deep, rich velvet cloak that took her into its folds and caressed her with infinite tenderness, infinite delight.

She was floating, sinking, turning, and the rest of the world was fading away, a soft background, like music, like the wind. She melted in his arms. There was no other word for it. Her body turned soft and pliant as wax in the sun and she flowed against his hard, male angles, fitting her curves to his design.

Never end, never end—she wanted the kiss to go on forever. It had everything, warmth, tenderness and a provocative touch of sexuality that seemed to bring her senses alive. His taste was minty fresh but rich as Belgian chocolate. His smell was male and musky, orange blossoms crushed against a masculine chest. Never end, never end. When he finally began to draw away from her, she found herself yearning toward his retreating face, as though she couldn't bear to ever be apart again.

Onlookers in the crowd at the entrance emitted a massive involuntary sigh.

"Wow," breathed the photographer.

"Wow," breathed Mason, staring down at her as though he'd never seen her before.

Trish couldn't say anything. Her body and soul were still in shock.

"Let's get out of here," Mason murmured, still holding her. "Come on."

Lacing his fingers through hers, he began to lead her down the parking strip toward the sea cliffs where the cypress grew flat and wild against the rocks. She followed, numb, not even looking back toward the captain's walk. The plan was out the window. Trish was going to have to play the rest of this scene as best she could without it.

Five

The marina was deserted. Everyone was up the hill at the clubhouse. Water lapped against the gently bobbing yachts and sea gulls screamed overhead. Trish leaned against the gate at the bottom of the ramp and wondered why she'd come.

The kiss. She shivered inside but hid it. The kiss had been what had done it—what had sent them on this wild chase down to the marina, away from the crowd. But the cool sea air had slapped some sense into her. And now she wished she were anywhere but here.

She glanced back at Mason. He was standing with his legs wide apart, his arms folded across his chest, his face in a reserved frown and his gaze on the horizon. She shivered again but not from exquisite memory this time.

She needed to get out of here. This had been a big mistake. Maybe she could plead temporary insanity and make good her escape.

She turned to face him, her back pressed to the mesh gate that led to the landing.

"Well, this is the marina," she said brightly. "Lovely, isn't it? I especially like the blue canvas against the white boats. It's so cheery." She made herself smile. "Now I suppose we ought to be getting back to the others, don't you think?"

Before she had a chance to take the first step, he moved forward and effectively blocked her. "Hold on, Trish," he said quietly. "Not so fast."

Her eyes were huge as she gazed up at him. The breeze was ruffling her copper hair and tossing the folds of her skirt around her knees. He hesitated, wondering why he always seemed to make the wrong moves when he was with her. Maybe that was because he wasn't sure what he wanted from her—what she wanted from him.

His jaw tightened. What was he doing out here anyway? This wasn't what he'd come to this party for. He had a job to do. He was starting a new life—and the first thing he did was go off like a flake with a pretty girl. Not the best way to make a first impression on the man he expected to work for.

But that kiss . . .

Inadvertently his gaze dropped to her lips and he felt a quick, urgent impulse to taste them again. Annoying, this temptation she represented. He thought he'd developed skills in being able to resist this sort of youthful adventure, but those skills seemed to desert him around Trish. If he weren't careful, he would end up doing something he would regret.

His gaze strayed back to her shining green eyes and he sighed, shaking his head ever so slightly. She was damn near irresistible—fresh and honest and full of life. She made him want to smile every time he looked at her.

He wasn't quite ready to head back to the party. There was no denying he enjoyed looking at Trish, enjoyed being with her. Maybe that was a part of his nature he would never be able to change. But there must be no more kissing.

"You've got some explaining to do before we go back," he reminded her. "Usually when I've been involved in an engagement, I've known about it ahead of time. This one's come as a bit of a shock."

"Oh." She couldn't tell if he were laughing or annoyed. It could make all the difference in how she approached this explanation. But whatever she said, it was bound to be a bit embarrassing.

"Well, you see, Howie...he took something I said the wrong way and assumed I was engaged, and since I was trying to get him to give up on thinking we could ever have any sort of relationship..."

"You opted for a quickie engagement as a convenient way out."

She nodded. "That's about it," she admitted. "I...I'm sorry. I didn't mean to get you involved...."

"No apology necessary. I've been engaged before. I can handle it."

She looked into his eyes but she still couldn't tell what he was thinking. Turning, she slipped past him, going back up the ramp. He followed, not protesting, as she turned away from the clubhouse, out along the boardwalk that skirted the edge of the water. They walked slowly side by side, with Trish letting her fingers trail lightly along the top of the restraining rail.

"Just how many engagements have you been in?" she asked, unable to hold back her curiosity.

"You mean before this one?" His tone was still ambiguous. "Let's just say I've toyed with the idea of marriage a few times."

"But had never gone through with it?" She turned to look at him, brushing the hair back out of her eyes.

"That's right."

Swinging to a stop she leaned out over the railing and looked into the slightly oily water again. He stopped beside her, leaning close by, his shoulders almost touching hers. She bit her lip, feeling his presence in a way that made her heart beat just a little faster.

She liked him. Heaven help her—she liked the man. And he was without a doubt the most exciting male she'd ever been this close to. Deliciously dangerous, that was what this was. Well, she was supposed to keep him occupied for a while. At least she was doing her job.

She looked at him and he gazed back. It was all right. His face was open right now. He was teasable. Maybe they could be friends. Maybe they could put that sense-provoking kiss behind them and go on to a light, friendly relationship that would put this all into proper perspective for them.

Taking the bit and running with it, she turned and threw him an impish grin. "Lots of engagements, but no marriages, huh? Why not? Are you allergic to orange blossoms? Or just too scared of commitment?"

Humor lines crinkled around his eyes. He was taking her nudges in the manner they were meant to be received. "I don't think 'scared' is the word to use, exactly."

"Too set in your stodgy old bachelor ways, perhaps? Too anxious to keep hold of that charming playboy freedom you thrive on?"

His eyebrows rose. "I'm thriving, am I? That's nice to know."

She nodded solemnly, looking him over. "Without a doubt." Her eyes narrowed. "Tell me about them."

"About whom?"

"Those women you almost married."

He grinned, his shoulders relaxing, his entire body returning to the lazy, fluid way he carried it so well. They were definitely comfortable with one another now. The tension was gone. "You don't want to know about them."

"Ah, that is where you're wrong. I want to know all about them." She bumped him with her shoulder, like a friend, a buddy. "And most of all, I want to know what they each did that finally sent you running in the opposite direction."

"What do you want to know that for?"

"Research. Pure research."

"Uh-huh." His eyes sparkled with humor. "Well, I'll tell you if you promise not to let it out. You see, each one of those poor, unfortunate ladies had the same secret vice. It's something generally not mentioned in polite society, so I'd appreciate it if you could keep it under wraps."

Her eyes widened. "You can count on me," she assured him. "What was it?"

He looked around as though to make sure no one could overhear them, then moved a bit closer, his shoulder rubbing against hers, and looked deeply into her eyes saying in a conspiratorial whisper, "Humming."

She blinked, not sure she'd heard correctly. "What?"

"Humming. They were all secret hummers, every one of them. I can't stand that." He shook his head in mock sorrow. "Humming is especially annoying when one is enjoying the tunes on an oldies station. If you want to sing along, fine. But humming..." He shuddered eloquently. "No, once I realized they were hummers, I had to terminate the relationships."

Trish forced back the grin that was threatening to take over her mouth. "I see," she said wisely.

He stared at her, his gaze intent. "You don't... hum...do you?"

Raising her hand like a Girl Scout taking the oath, she shook her head. "Never. I wouldn't think of it."

His smile was sunny. "Great. Then we should have no problem at all."

Her eyes laughed back at him. "Perfect."

"Which brings us back to the matter at hand. Just what do we do now that we are engaged, anyway? What are our plans for the future?"

She lifted her chin, her eyes glittering challengingly. "Trying to beg off now, are you?"

His grin was slow but sure. He'd turned toward her in his lazy, sleepy way that seemed to act as a drug on her senses, and his dark-eyed gaze took her in and held her as surely as if he'd wrapped her in his strong arms. "Not on your life," he drawled, reaching out to touch her cheek lightly with three fingers. "In fact, this time, I just might let the thing run its course and find out what happens next."

This was ample evidence of why he was considered a ladies' man. His charm was all part of his standard act, and she knew it. And yet she couldn't treat it with the contempt it deserved. In fact, she had to admit, she was enjoying it.

"Hah," she said faintly but with spirit. "That'll be the day."

"What makes you say that?"

"You'll never get married."

"How can you be so sure?"

"You have too much fun twisting every available female around your little finger, that's how." She tossed her head and started walking again. It was true, what she'd said, and the thought was freeing somehow. She could be herself with this man. She didn't have to worry about what he thought, because he lived life on surfaces. Funny. His lack of depth could let her open up to him. It didn't make sense, but it was true.

He quickly fell in beside her. "And what about you, Trish?" he asked, glancing at her sideways. "What keeps you from getting married?"

The question startled her. No teasing answer came readily to mind, so she found herself answering as honestly as she could. "Marriage is so important. I mean, the health and future of an entire family is built on the marriage. It's vital to make sure that foundation is firm. I guess I haven't gotten married because I still haven't found a man who would be right to help form that foundation."

When he answered Mason's voice was surprisingly harsh with a thread of sarcasm barely discernible. "I see. The perfect man. Just plain old love isn't enough. Is that it?"

They'd come to the end of the boardwalk. She turned and looked at him.

"Is it enough for you?" she asked simply.

She had him there. How was he to know? He'd never been in love. Not really. The engagements had been experiments that hadn't panned out. Every time he'd fallen crazy in "love," it had only taken a few days to reverse the emotion completely and show him just how little he could stand the thought of sharing his life with just one woman.

"You take marriage too seriously," he said instead of answering. "After all, what is it? Just two people giving a relationship a try. If it works out, great. If not, they each have the right to move on to something else. It's as simple as that."

She flushed quickly. The urge to argue rose in her throat, but she forced it back. She knew he was referring back to her parents' marriage again. She didn't want to talk about that.

She glanced back at the marina, then spun and put a hand up to shade her eyes, looking out over the bay, then to the promontory just off to the right. Childhood memories stirred, sunny days and laughter and picnics on the beach. Remembered joy flowed through her and she smiled, turning back to Mason.

"Would you like to visit a magic place?" she asked him, her eyes alight with anticipation.

His slow smile was reluctant. "What are you talking about?" he asked skeptically.

She grabbed his hand and tugged. "Come on! I haven't gone in years, but we used to play there when we were children. Come on." She turned toward the bluff half a football field length away across the beach.

His fingers slipped around her wrist and pulled back, resisting. "Wait a minute," he said, amusement in his voice. "You can't wear those little high heels out in the sand."

She looked down at her feet in frustration. "You're right." Not hesitating a moment, she kicked them off and reached up under her skirt to begin to roll down her panty hose.

His eyebrows arched in amazement. "What are you doing?"

She grinned up at him from her contorted position. "Reverting to childhood," she said happily. "Come on. Take off your shoes and socks and come with me."

"Back into childhood?" he asked wryly. But he sank down to sit on the edge of the boardwalk and began to do as she'd urged.

Straightening, she pushed her shoes into pockets she found at her hips in the skirt, along with her rolled-up panty hose. Then she knelt before him and began folding up the cuffs of his wool trousers, chattering as she worked.

"You'll love this place. It's an estuary—like finding a tropical island. No one ever goes there, you can't get to it from the road. You have to go through the secret passageway." She grinned up at him again. "My friends and I used to put traps around the entrance so that no one would ever dare go in there but us."

Mason didn't think he'd had a woman rolling up his pant legs since he was a little boy and his sister Charity had adjusted hand-me-down pants to fit him. He watched Trish, bemused, wondering how she could go from the sort of anger and hurt he'd witnessed in her to this utter lack of self-consciousness she was displaying now.

"We're not going to have to crawl through mud and spiders, are we?" he asked distastefully.

She laughed. "Chicken!" She bounced to her feet and began to dance across the sand. "Come on! It's a wonderful place. There are frogs and egrets and blue herons and spotted turtles and wild blackberries growing along the banks. Oh, I hope they're ripe! It'll be worth it, believe me."

He followed her, feeling strangely more adult as she became more childlike. She was surprising him. He'd known she was special from the very first, but this capacity for happiness was unexpected. Unexpected, and very attractive.

"Once, Shelley and I found a blue heron's nest," she remembered as he came beside her. "We hid in the cattails and watched while the mother tried to feed the baby birds. Their feet were so big, they kept getting them tangled and falling on their beaks. We got stomachaches trying so hard not to laugh and scare them."

He could picture the two of them crouched in the marshes and suddenly knew it was a time she looked back on as golden, when her mother and father seemed happy and life seemed secure. Was that why she was so full of anticipation? Did she think she could recapture that feeling in her hidden, enchanted place?

"It's in around here," she said as they approached the bluff and she began to push back brush in order to find the obscure entrance. "At least I thought it was. They couldn't have filled it in, could they?"

Mason pushed back a branch and found a gap between two large rocks. "Is this it?"

She whirled and cried, "Yes!" and they started through, stretching themselves taller and thinner to squeeze between the boulders and pass into the cave. It was dark for only a moment, but Trish took Mason's hand as though to guide him, making him smile. The sand in the cave was cold on their bare feet. And then they had broken through to the other side and had to clamber over breakdown to get into the canyon that held Trish's enchanted estuary.

She climbed down backward and looked up to see Mason paused above her. The look on his face told her something was wrong. She landed on her feet and spun around, and for just a moment, she thought they'd come to the wrong place.

There were no cattails, no meandering rivulets of water, no frogs, no blue herons. Instead there was the shell of a large building, with tinted windows already fixed in place and electrical wiring hanging loose. Stark, newly-laid concrete driveways and empty parking lots filled the space where back bay life had once thrived. A road cut had been blasted through the far cliff, and a paved road led back to the coast highway. Condos. They were building condominiums where her enchanted estuary used to be.

For a moment she stood very still, stunned. Then slowly, jerkily, she moved forward, as though she had to touch the building to make sure it was real. She still couldn't believe it. How could this have happened? Why hadn't she known? Why hadn't she paid more attention to the newspapers? Why hadn't she done something to stop it?

Mason watched her go, watched her touch the wooden framing, the glass window. She walked around the building and looked on the other side, to see, he was sure, if any of her marshes were left at all. He could tell by the way she turned back, her shoulders sagging, that everything was gone.

He waited while she walked back to stand beside him. Her misery was palpable. Tears glistened in her eyes, though she seemed to be doing her best to hold them back. He didn't know what he could do to comfort her, and the helpless feeling built into frustration. For a moment, he was angry—angry at himself for not being more help, angry at her for being so damn vulnerable, for not facing reality, for letting things hurt her so badly.

"I hate change," she said, her voice choked and wavering.

He wanted to turn on her, yell, tell her to grow up. Instead he cleared his throat and said gruffly, "All things must change or die, Trish. You know that." Shoving his hands into the pockets of his trousers, he stared out toward where the water lapped against the shore and cursed himself for not taking her in his arms. Did her sorrow embarrass him? He wasn't sure. But he knew it disturbed him, and he knew he wasn't good at dealing with this sort of emotionalism.

Trish had turned and was looking at him with a frown. "'Change or die'?" she echoed scornfully. "Isn't that just a bit melodramatic?"

Swinging back to face her glare, he shook his head. "Not at all. Life is growth. Growth is change. Change is inevitable."

"So is smog. That doesn't mean I have to like it."

"Who said you have to like it? But you do have to accept it."

"No." Her eyes glittered with challenge now. "I don't have to do any such thing. I'm . . . I'm going to write to the paper, get a picket line together, sue the contractor!"

"Hire yourself a skywriter," he continued for her just a bit mockingly. "March on Washington, bomb the building. That ought to do the blue herons a lot of good."

Her eyes wavered and her anger deflated. "I guess it's a little late, isn't it?"

"I think so."

She bit her lip. At least her eyes were no longer rimmed with tears. Mason felt rather pleased with himself. Maybe he knew more about comforting than he'd thought. Get her angry. Make her laugh. That was the answer.

"I still hate change," she muttered stubbornly, glaring at the construction as though just her energy could blast it away.

"Change is what we're stuck with," he said in return. "Just look at us. Our relationship has done nothing but change from the first time we met."

She sighed. "And you like that?"

"I didn't say I liked it. It's just the way it is. Look at how you distrusted me at first. Then you hated me."

"I did not!"

He shrugged. "You did a good imitation. Then..." He touched her chin with one finger and gave her a slow smile. "Then you kind of liked me—that afternoon at the pool."

She flushed, remembering. "That...that was a mistake."

He grinned, his fingers fanning out to caress her cheek as she looked up at him. "Right. A mistake." His gaze settled on her lips, then moved lazily back to meet her green eyes. "Then today you set it up so I would have to kiss you."

Her eyes widened in horror. "I did no such thing!"

He shrugged, moving closer, enjoying the way the breeze ruffled her hair, the way her fresh scent filled his senses. "It wasn't me who spread that story about us being engaged," he said softly. "You got your kiss, Trish. Was it all that you expected? Or were you disappointed?"

The background was fading away and all her aware-
ness was centered on him. "I...no, it was just...fine."

"Fine? Only fine?" He touched her feather-soft hair,
letting it tickle his fingertips, then curled his hand
around her ear. "I think we should kiss again, just to
find out if that's changed."

His touch was turning her knees to water. She shook
her head. "No," she said hoarsely. "I . . . I don't think
we should."

He raised one eyebrow in question. "Why not?"

She licked her lips and tried to force herself to pull
away. But she couldn't. It was as though he had her in
a spell. "You kiss funny," she said in desperation.

His head jerked back and he stared at her, his hand
still in her hair. "What?"

That had been a stupid thing to say. She wasn't sure
how she was going to get out of this one. Nothing came
to mind and she merely stared back at him, appalled at
her own tactlessness.

"You don't like the way I kiss?" he was asking her,
actually looking offended. It was obvious no woman
had ever said such a thing to him before.

"I didn't say I didn't like it." She searched her mind
but couldn't think of a thing to add.

"But you said I kiss funny."

"I meant...it made me feel funny." No, this was
worse. She should learn to say nothing if she had nothing intelligent to say.

At least the laughter was back in his gaze. And his
fingers spread against the side of her head, making her
want to nestle her face in the palm of his hand. "Trish,
darling," he said with soft humor, bending near. "If
this is the first time a kiss has made you feel—quote—

funny—unquote—I think we may have made a break-through here.''

He was going to kiss her again. Trish's heartbeat was quickening. She knew what this was. She had no illusions. He was a playboy. He kissed women as casually as she poured herself a glass of milk every evening. It meant nothing at all. But she didn't care. She swayed toward him and his arms came around her.

The intensity of her response took her breath away. His large, powerful body held hers in an embrace that gave her a feeling of protection she'd never had before. And at the same time his hands trailed across her skin, tantalizing, setting her senses ablaze with longing.

Her head fell back and his mouth closed on hers, hot and exciting. All reality fell away. Nothing mattered but the places where his body touched hers, and his mouth mattered most of all. His heat poured into her—golden, sundrenched, making her gasp with wonder. The magic was still there. She'd never known a man's kiss to be so awe inspiring.

Images swirled in her head, images of crashing waves and summer storm clouds, of suntan lotion being rubbed on satin skin, of sun-baked bodies entangled in the sand. Her muscles seemed to melt away, leaving only his arms to support her. She felt as though she could stay here forever, locked in his care, caught in the whirlpool of his sensuality.

When they finally drew apart she felt like a swimmer coming up for air, her lungs about to burst. They stood very close for the next few moments, both breathing hard, gazes caught in mutual wonder.

''How do you do that?'' he asked her softly.

She stared, not sure if he were teasing her, or what he meant if he were serious. He couldn't possibly have been swept up in the magic the way she had been. Could he? "Do what?" she asked breathlessly.

But he only shook his head, his hands caressing her shoulders. "Did you feel 'funny' this time?" he asked softly.

She dropped her gaze in embarrassment. "That's none of your business."

His hands moved to hold her face as though it were a precious work of art, making her look back up, and his gaze deepened. "I want to make you feel 'funny,' Trish," he murmured, his face coming near hers again. "I want . . ."

A sudden wave of panic swept through Trish and she pulled away, avoiding his gaze.

"We'd better get back," she said quickly. She stared at him, putting her fingers on her face where his hand had been. He was much too much for her, and she knew it. She turned and took one last look at the monstrosity that had been plunked down on top of her childhood memories. "Come on."

He watched her start back through the cave, thinking how very good she had felt in his arms, thinking he wanted her there again—soon. But why had it been this way? Why hadn't he been able to take her in his arms for simple comfort—why had he needed to turn it into romance and sex in order to open up to her that much? He'd never realized before that he had this inability to deal with sadness and loss on a human scale—that he needed to turn it into a man-woman thing in order to handle it. He was going to have to think this through. When had he lost the capacity to reach out to another human on a normal level?

But her kiss had been worth waiting for. Even though coming here with her had shattered all his good intentions, it had been worth it. This was one woman he didn't want to let out of his sight for long.

They walked back without the happy anticipation they'd come with. But the mood between them was warm, warm and close. They talked softly on their trek, teased one another, laughed. It seemed natural for Mason to put his arm around her shoulders as they reached the start of the boardwalk. Trish smiled when he did it.

People were beginning to flock down to the marina from the clubhouse. It was almost time for the yachts to begin coming in. But they hardly noticed, still involved in their conversation, until Shelley came toward them, marching smartly across the boardwalk.

"Where have you been?" she demanded when she was in hearing range. "You've been gone forever."

"We went to the cove," Trish began, ready to launch into her outrage about the development going on there. But Shelley didn't give her a chance. Frowning down at their sandy bare feet, she shook her head.

"Well, Trish, you've done your job perfectly well, but Mom and Dad were playing off a different script. Things are going from bad to worse. They had a tremendous fight and now everyone is choosing sides. It's awful. You've got to come back in and help me pick up the pieces."

Trish felt sick. She'd been so sure all they needed was a chance to be together and everything would be all right again. Was it hopeless? No, never that. She glanced at Mason and suddenly realized he was looking at her with growing suspicion in his eyes.

"Job?" he muttered. "What does she mean by that?"

Oh, Lord. Trish looked from Mason to her sister and back again. Oh, Lord, don't let Shelley say anything that will . . .

"Thanks for cooperating, Mason," Shelley was saying firmly, ignoring the warning flashed from Trish's eyes. "Trish volunteered to keep you out of the way for a while so that we could try to give our parents a chance to get back together again. It didn't work." She shrugged. "That's the way it goes. Maybe next time." Turning, she strode on back toward the clubhouse, leaving them behind.

Trish felt a headache beginning right where happiness had been throbbing only moments before. How could everything seem so right one moment, so wrong the next?

Mason was staring at her as though he could hardly believe what he'd just heard. "I see," he said coldly. "So the whole thing was a setup from the start." His gaze was savagely cynical. "Everything, including the kiss. Is that it?"

She put a hand to her head and sighed. She could deny it, make excuses, find rationalizations. She could shout back at him. But what good would that do? Her parents were still apart. She'd been out kissing this playboy while her parents' lives were being shattered even further. She turned toward him, exasperated. "Oh, come on, Mason," she snapped. "Cut the outrage. You're the ladies' man. Surely you can take it."

He stared at her, anger building. He knew about using people. He'd been guilty of that particular sin a time or two in the past. But the thought that she had been using him, that she had lured him out to the marina, not because she wanted to be with him, but because she wanted to keep him out of the way, was infuriating. And even more infuriating was the realization that he had fallen for it, hook, line and sinker. He'd actually been convincing himself that she was special, not like other women. And all the time she'd only been hiding her contempt for him.

"It's always the innocent-looking ones who turn out to have the hidden agenda," he said bitterly. "When were you going to let me know I was just a pawn in your game?"

He turned away before she had a chance to answer. After all he had his own agenda, one he'd been ignoring for too long. "Never mind, Trish," he called back as he left her. "I've got work to do. It's been fun. See you around some time."

She watched him go and wondered why it hurt to see him angry. She should have told him she was sorry—but right now her emotions were in such turmoil she wasn't sure what she was thinking or feeling.

He'd said some things to her that she was saving to ponder later when she was alone. And at the same time, she knew it was no use to think of them. You couldn't take anything that he said seriously. He'd said it all before so many times. Of course, he was just a playboy.

That was over. It was time to get back to the real problem—her parents and their deteriorating marriage. Turning she saw her mother coming down the ramp, arm in arm with Bert, and she sighed.

Good old Bert. Maybe he could get the two of them back together after all. He was her father's best friend. And her mother's too, when it came right down to it. She had to get herself to a powder room in the club, freshen her makeup, put on her hose and get down to business. There was plenty of work to be done.

There were shouts as the yachts began to come in, but Trish hardly heard them. As the crowd poured down the walkways and ramp toward the marina, she was walking the opposite way, her thoughts as heavy as her footsteps.

Six

———

I swear, Trish, that man at the table by the window keeps staring at you. If you're not interested, I just might start flirting with him myself.''

Trish kept her attention on the salad on the plate before her. She knew who it was in the window seat. She'd seen him when she and her friend Carla had walked into the crowded restaurant, and she'd almost tugged on Carla's arm and suggested they find another place to eat. But in the end, she'd decided not to do that. She couldn't let him see that he still affected her in any way. Not after all this time.

It had been over four months since that day at the Regatta, when she'd taken him to her secret cove and lost her head over his magic kisses. She'd managed to avoid him ever since, even though he was working for her mother and Bert in some new business they were starting up, a venture she didn't like to think about or hear about.

Her parents were still separated—another subject she preferred to ignore. At first she had worked so hard, finding excuses to throw the two of them together, trying to talk to them separately, then in a conference between the three of them that quickly became a shouting match with Trish as the helpless referee. That was when she had realized that a reconciliation was going to have to come from them. The more she pushed, the more they resisted.

So she gave up on the matchmaking and was letting things run their course, hoping against hope that they would come to their senses on their own. It was beginning to look like a very long wait.

"I wish you would turn around and just look at him once," Carla was saying, peeking across the room through a curtain of ash blond hair that swept across her forehead and fell to her shoulders. "He's so handsome. And he's got that sexy gleam in his eye. You know what I mean?"

Did she ever. She didn't have to turn around to see it. That gleam had haunted her dreams for months now.

"Ignore him," she advised, spearing a long piece of jicama with her fork. "He'll get tired of staring soon enough."

Carla apparently couldn't fathom this casual disregard for the attentions of an attractive man. "Trish, really. I'll bet he knows you or something. Just turn around and take one quick look."

It was obvious Carla wasn't going to give up until Trish had acknowledged Mason's presence. She turned slowly, met Mason's dark gaze, and nodded. He raised his wineglass. She half smiled and turned back again.

"Oh, wow, you do know him, don't you? Who is he? What's his name?"

Trish could foresee a long, awkward session of questions and answers if she didn't nip this in the bud. "Carla, I'd rather not talk about him."

"But why not?"

Trish hesitated, then plunged in. What the heck. Carla was a sweetheart, but in this case, she was asking for it. "We were engaged once," she said softly. Well, it was almost true. "It...it was very brief." Hardly more than an hour or so, in fact. "We were torn apart by circumstances." His pigheadedness—my carelessness. "One thing led to another." He stuck out his pride and I trampled on it. "And suddenly, it was over."

Carla's eyes were full of pity. "Oh, you poor baby. He's so...so..."

Yes, he was, but he was also the sort of playboy a serious woman didn't need in her life. "I really don't want to talk about it, Carla."

Her friend nodded sympathetically. "I know. It hurts too much, doesn't it?" She reached out and took Trish's hand and suddenly the light of inspiration filled her blue eyes. "Maybe I could help you. I could be a go-between. I could talk to him...."

Trish had to work hard to keep from groaning aloud. "Carla, please. It's over, and that's the way I want it. Please, let's drop the subject."

It only occurred to her for a split second or two that she was echoing the exact words her mother used every time Trish tried to bring up ways for her to reconcile with her husband. But she dismissed those similarities out of hand. This was completely different, of course.

The fact was, just being in the same room with Mason was affecting her ability to think clearly. More than once she found herself staring at Carla without the slightest idea what her friend had been saying. Her attention had been hijacked by a man in a window seat, a man she never wanted to see again.

"Well, I really do need to get back to the store," she said suddenly. "We're getting in a shipment of stickers today, and if I'm not there to supervise, Wendy will take two cases of everything. She can't resist stickers."

She gathered together her purse and parcels and stood, barely noticing Carla's startled expression, because her whole being was focused on the moment she would turn and meet Mason's eyes again.

She turned. She looked. And what met her gaze was an empty chair and a busboy clearing away the remains of a mushroom omelet, some sourdough rolls and a glass of wine.

She'd been dreading the moment she would have to walk by him, and now that it had come, he was gone, and a feeling of such loss, such devastation swept over her, she had to sit back down in her chair until it passed.

She quickly rationalized the feelings away and shoved thoughts of Mason to the back of her mind. She was too busy to think about him anyway. Business was booming in her shop and she was implementing a new art section, hiring student artists to come in and personalize items she sold in her store on a custom basis. The reaction had been enthusiastic and she was caught up in plans, so there was little time to think of things that might have been.

Over the next few weeks she caught glimpses of Mason here and there, once from her mother's apartment when he was sunning himself in the courtyard below, and another time she saw him walking along Balboa Boulevard with Howie, of all people, as she was driving by in her car. They both waved. She waved back. And she rode on, mulling over the possibilities of that relationship.

It wasn't until sometime later, at a Chamber of Commerce mixer, that she actually spoke to him again.

She arrived late, in the middle of the speaker's presentation. Already self-conscious about her tardiness, she had to pass back and forth between tables looking for a seat, and when she finally found a vacancy, she sat down and realized with a start that the speaker was Mason. The discovery came as such a shock, she never did find out what his topic was.

She could hardly reconcile this man with the barefooted beachboy she'd first met in her mother's apartment. That Mason had been sexy but seemingly insubstantial. This Mason had lost none of his sensual luster, but had added a sense of dignity and command that she would hardly have thought possible. He looked like a captain of industry rather than a ski bum. How had he done that?

His presentation was over. People were applauding and many were rising to surround him and ask questions as he tried to leave the podium. Trish sat very still, watching, wondering, and then a voice muttered very near her right ear.

"I want that man."

Trish turned, startled, and found she had chosen a seat next to Brigitte Holloway, socialite and owner of Brigitte's Travel World, and a stunning example of the human species in her own right.

Brigitte's long, elegant hand with its persimmon-colored nails and blinding array of diamonds reached out and circled Trish's wrist, demanding attention. Her gaze was fixed on Mason.

"I want that man," she said even more firmly. Brigitte had a reputation for getting what she wanted.

Trish looked at Mason, then back at the woman next to her. She and Brigitte had known one another forever but had never been particularly friendly. Trish was sure this was no personal confession meant just for her. Brigitte was merely stating a goal. Any audience would have done.

She looked at Mason again and shuddered slightly. "I...I don't think he's your type." Why had she said that? He was exactly Brigitte's type. But her statement had the effect of turning Brigitte's brilliant green gaze on her.

"You know him?" she demanded.

"I...well, I've met him...."

The fingers tightened on her wrist. "Take me to him. Introduce me."

The next thing Trish knew, she was in line to speak to Mason with Brigitte hanging on her arm and her conscience in outraged turmoil. She didn't want to talk to Mason. She certainly didn't want to put Brigitte in his lap. What was she doing here? She looked around longingly at the exit, but Brigitte's fingers were as unyielding as a vise.

"Hello, Trish."

They had made it to the head of the line. In fact, they were all that was left of the line. She hesitated, afraid to speak. What if her voice wavered? What if he could see how shaky he made her?

His dark eyes were unreadable but she had the distinct impression he was glad to see her. And suddenly that made it easier.

"Hello, Mason. How have you been?"

"Fine. Thriving, in fact."

He looked as though he were waiting to see if she would smile at that reference to their conversation that day at the cove, but it took her just a beat too long to realize what he was referring to, and when she did, the moment had passed.

"I guess the business is doing quite well then," she said quickly instead.

He nodded. "You should come by and see what we're doing. Your mother would like that."

Of course. What was wrong with her? Why hadn't she done so before this? Because she thought the business, whatever exactly it was, was merely a stopgap, a hobby, something to keep her mother occupied until she went back to be a full-time wife to her father again. But it had been so long now. She really should go by and see what was up. She opened her mouth, ready to make a date to do just that when she received a sharp, jabbing elbow in the side, reminding her of what she'd come for.

"Oh. Uh...Mason, I'd like you to meet Brigitte Holloway of Brigitte's Travel World."

"Mason Ames, I'm so pleased to meet you." Brigitte took his hand and looked as though she would probably never let go of it again. She was a beautiful woman and her smile would have dazzled sterner stuff than Mason. But studying his reaction, Trish wasn't sure just what he thought.

"Cancel your current travel agent. I'm prepared to make you an offer you can't refuse."

Mason looked bemused. "We don't have a travel agent yet. We don't do a lot of traveling, and I don't foresee..."

"No one ever does, believe me. But I can read the signs. I know a winner when I see one. You will grow, you will prosper, and before you know it, you'll need to visit suppliers, canvas clients, attend conventions. You'll need me, darling, and that is what I live for, to be needed by my own special, special customers.''

Mason was beginning to glow under the warmth of her flattery. What man, Trish fumed to herself, wouldn't?

Brigitte gazed soulfully into his dark eyes and declared, ''When you think of luxury, when you think of being pampered until you can't stand it any longer, I want you to think of me. I want to take care of you. I want to make sure you sleep on satin sheets. I want only tower suites for you, with croissants on a tray in the morning and a spa at your disposal. I want every detail of every moment of every trip to be memorable.'' She pulled his hand over her heart. ''When can we get together for lunch to discuss the arrangements?''

Mason glanced at Trish's hostile gaze and grinned. ''How about today? I'm free.''

Brigitte seemed to be transported with ecstasy. ''Wonderful! Oh, I can hardly wait. I'll pick you up at your office at . . .'' She snapped out her wrist to give a sharp look at her watch. ''Shall we say, twelvish?''

''Twelvish it is.'' He turned back to Trish and grinned again. ''Don't you want to shower me with offers, too?'' he asked hopefully.

She glared right back. ''I'd rather shower you with something cold and wet,'' she muttered. ''I think you're going to need it.''

He laughed softly, nodded to Brigitte, and excused himself.

''Thanks,'' Brigitte told her frankly. ''I owe you one.'' She sighed. ''I'm going to go home and get ready for lunch. I want to look my very best for this one.''

The thought of this woman in Mason's arms sent a knife through Trish's heart. She could hardly stand it. Did she have any right to complain? Of course not, none at all. But she still hated the idea and suddenly a thought occurred to her.

"You know, Brigitte," she said to the woman. "I should give you a little advice about Mason. I know something about his likes and dislikes—and there is one thing that really turns him on in a woman."

Brigitte was all ears. "Well, give! What is it?"

Trish took a deep breath, feeling like a heel, but determined. "Humming," she said firmly. "He can't resist a woman who hums along to music." It was a long shot. After all he'd used the humming thing as a joke, really. But one never knew...

Brigitte looked thoughtful. "Humming, huh? I'll practice up on that, too." She waved merrily at Trish. "Toodle-oo. Wish me luck." And then she was gone.

Trish watched her go with chagrin, wishing she'd sat somewhere else in the restaurant, wishing she'd never laid eyes on Brigitte and her travel folders. Turning she found herself face-to-face with Mason, who either hadn't walked away after all or had come back. The look on his face told her he'd heard every word, and her cheeks turned bright red in the time it took to realize that fact. His eyes were laughing, but he didn't say a word, and she left as fast as she could, cursing herself for every misstep of the morning.

She mulled things over for a few days and then called Shelley. She knew her sister was keeping closer tabs on their mother lately and she wanted an update before she ventured out.

"This new business Mom has started? What is it exactly?"

There was a pause on the other end of the line. "You haven't been by to see it yet?"

"No. Just what is it that they are making? I was under the impression that it still had something to do with surfing. What is it, shorts and tops? Mom's been talking about starting a clothing line for years."

Another pause and then Shelley's tentative voice. "I think you should come by and see for yourself. It's really an exciting project. I've been doing some part-time work for Mom and Bert, some bookkeeping. Mom and Bert have leased that building over on the corner of Seascape and Balboa. They're there all the time. Drop by some afternoon."

Mom and Bert, Mom and Bert. Something in the sound of that pairing was beginning to rub her the wrong way.

"Great. I'll do that," she said to Shelley. But inside something was rebelling, something was resisting like a petulant child resisted bedtime. It was the same little something that made her change the subject every time her mother tried to talk about the new business. The same little something that made her mind switch off when the topic was raised by anyone else. She didn't want there to be a real, growing and prospering business that didn't include her father. Instinctively she knew that the more successful the business was, the more it pulled her mother away from the marriage and out into the wide open world.

Her father seemed happy enough, but she knew that was all surface. He refused to talk about her mother at all. But there was not much new in that. All he had ever wanted to talk about was business. No change there.

She knew she would have to go over and see this new venture but she put it off. It nagged at her like an upcoming dental appointment, something she dreaded in a dull, unthinking way. Any day now she would take care of that little detail in her life. Any day now.

It was only a week later that her mother called to invite her out to lunch. Trish had high hopes that Laura was going to give her good news, but it turned out to be anything but.

"I've filed for divorce, Trish," her mother told her gently. "I know this is going to upset you. But it was something I had to do. I hope you'll understand."

Trish most emphatically did not understand, but she was beginning to learn to keep her emotions more hidden from the others.

"Does Daddy know?"

"Yes. He and I have talked the whole thing out."

Trish cringed inside, but she hid it. "All I ask is that you think everything through, Mom," she said calmly. "Don't do anything hastily. Don't act in anger."

Her mother's look was troubled. "Trish . . ." She'd been about to tell her something, but she quickly changed her mind, shaking her head and laughing softly. "Oh, Trish, you're such a little bulldog. You can't let go of anything, can you?"

Trish didn't know what she meant and she was rather hurt by that characterization. But she knew there wasn't much she could do to stop her mother from filing for divorce. All she could do was pray something would happen to wake the two of them up before it became final.

The next time she saw Mason he was riding high, but not in the business sense. Trish was out for her usual early morning jog, and this time she'd chosen a run along a beach that was open to surfers from dawn until eight o'clock. She rarely paid much attention to surfers. They were usually too far out in the waves to see clearly. But for some reason she noticed a pair of familiar-looking bodies separate themselves from the neoprene-clad crowd and try for a singularly spectacular swell that quickly turned into a monster wave.

Trish paused in horrified fascination as she watched one of the boards catapult toward the sun while the surfer's body flew in the opposite direction. Something about the way the body twisted before it plunged into the swirling waters looked recognizable.

"Mason?" she said aloud, incredulous.

She waited, breath held, for him to surface again, hardly noticing that his partner had caught the wave beautifully and was crusing toward her now, still hanging ten.

"Hey!" It was Howie. She blinked twice, just in case, but it definitely was Howie. "Hi!" He jumped off the board, flipping it up at the same time so that it landed handily in his reach. Very smooth, very professional. Howie was a born surfer. "What are you doing here?"

Considering her jogging shorts and running shoes, it shouldn't have been too difficult for him to draw his own conclusions, but Trish ignored that and turned her attention back to the waves.

"Is that Mason Ames out there?"

"Yup." Howie turned back toward the ocean, shading his eyes with one hand. "Where'd he go?"

"I don't know. I saw him wipe out and then he disappeared." Her anxiety was beginning to strain her voice. "You've got to go back out there and find him!"

"Here's his board." Howie sloshed back into the water to pull the neon-yellow-and-pink creation up onto the sand, turning it carefully for a full examination. "It looks okay."

"Who cares about the board!" Trish was beginning to think about kicking off her shoes and jumping into the brine herself. "Mason might be drowning out there. Will you go back out and—"

Howie grinned at her. "Aw, that's cute. You're really worried, aren't you? Hey, he's not a professional, but he's no gremmie, either."

First she would strangle Howie, then she would swim quickly out to the wave line and begin to dive for Mason's body. That was the plan formulating in her mind when a dark head bobbing a hundred yards offshore caught her eye.

"There he is." Relief flooded her so strongly her eyes began to sting. "He's all right!" Quickly she turned her face away so that Howie wouldn't see the moisture in her eyes. What an idiot. She had no idea why she was reacting so strongly.

"Of course he's all right." Howie grinned, oblivious. "Hey, Trish. Listen, I just want to say that I think it is really, really noble of you, this thing you're doing for Mason."

A shiver of wary alarm spread through her and she turned back to stare at him. "What, exactly, is it that I'm doing for him, Howie?"

"Why, the way you're staying away from him for six months, even though the two of you are engaged. Not many fiancées would be so understanding."

She blinked. Had Mason really continued her coverup so handily? "Did he . . . did he tell you why he needed me to stay away from him?"

"Sure. He needs the slack to get a foothold in the new business. I know all about it."

Mason never stopped surprising her. She watched him limp in toward shore and felt a warmth in her chest.

He looked at her from under eyelashes studded with diamonds of water. Then he sighed and came to a staggering halt before her. "This stuff is hard work. I'm dead."

He looked awfully good for a dead man, his hair black and matted against his head, his shoulders wide in the black neoprene wet suit cut off above the elbows and knees.

"What exactly are the two of you trying to prove?" she asked in her best schoolmarm tone.

Howie unzipped his wet suit and emerged, kicking it aside into the sand. "I'm teaching Mason how to surf," he said sunnily. "We're getting to be really good buddies."

Mason's head came up and he glared at his so-called friend. "I know how to surf," he growled malevolently. "I just had an unlucky spill out there."

Trish couldn't hide her smile. "From what I saw, you really could use some of Howie's expertise," she advised. "Howie is one of the very best."

Howie agreed with that, nodding happily. "He thinks, just because he's practically a champion skiier or something he should be able to surf just as good right from the get-go."

Mason swayed in the breeze but held his ground. "I surfed when I was a kid in Hawaii," he insisted, then added rather plaintively, "I don't remember it taking this much out of me in those days."

Howie made a face, then tried to make Mason feel better. "They say you never forget how to ride a bicycle, but maybe it's different with a surfboard," he placated.

Mason's eyes blazed and his teeth clenched. If he'd only had the strength, Trish could see he would have

gone for Howie's throat. Hiding her laughter she got
between them, just in case.

"Here, let me help you with that wet suit," she offered before she thought. It wasn't until she was reaching for the tab on the big zipper that ran from his
neckline to the crotch of the suit that she realized what
she was letting herself in for. She'd done it a thousand
times for other surfers straggling in exhausted from the
sea. She'd done it all her life. But something told her
this would be different. She hesitated and found him
watching her.

"Thanks," he said softly. "That would be nice."

There was no way to get out of it now. Gritting her
teeth, she took hold of the tab and began to yank it
down. It didn't come easily. And with each yank
another bit of his gorgeous body was exposed as the two
sides of the suit folded open, revealing his bare chest.

Drops of water fell from his hair and sparkled on his
warm brown shoulders. Her fingers were shaking, but
she had to tug so hard on the zipper, maybe he didn't
notice. Removing a body from a wet suit was a lot like
freeing someone from a coating of crazy glue. This
body, though, was worth the effort.

In the midst of the project Howie called over, "Hey
you guys, I'm going on up to the van. See you later."
And he began to trek off through the sand.

Trish didn't look up from her task. Mason merely
grunted. In moments the two of them were alone on the
deserted stretch of beach, except for the surfers out on
the waves.

She pulled back once the opening had uncovered his
navel. "You can do the rest," she said nervously, then
met his gaze and found his dark eyes were laughing at
her.

"What's the matter, Trish? Are you scared of me?" he asked, his voice soft but mocking.

"Of course not," she returned.

"Then why can't you finish what you started?"

He was manipulating her and she knew it. It worked. Challenged, she reached out and took hold of the tab again, giving a vicious yank that pulled it all the way down between his legs and let the suit fall all the way open. Jerking back her hand as though she'd scalded it, she looked up and found herself laughing right along with Mason, and then, found herself in his arms.

The wet suit had dropped to the sand, leaving Mason clad only in a tight, bright blue Lycra swimsuit. The sun was warm on the back of her head but his skin was cool. She could hardly breathe.

"That was very nice of you to help me," he murmured, his eyes warm with something that looked very much like affection. Or was it amusement? She wasn't really sure.

"I'm a nice person," she reminded him, standing very still, not wanting to give him an excuse to laugh at her as he would if she tried to get away from him.

"A very nice person," he agreed. "A very pretty person." He pulled her closer. "A very sexy person."

She tried to smile but it was wobbly. "They all say that," she managed to warble out.

His breath was warm on her face. "In fact, I think you're so nice, you deserve a reward."

"Oh . . . no, not really. . . ."

"Yes, really." His grin had a wicked edge to it. "But since I don't have any money with me, I'm afraid all I have to give you is . . . a kiss."

Trish squirmed, but she didn't really fight very hard. "Not here. It's . . . so public."

"Do you think the sea gulls will be offended?"

No, she didn't really think that. In fact it was hard to think of anything else but Mason while he held her so closely, his heart pounding against hers, his breath smelling so sweet.

"Or is it the kiss you're trying to get out of? Do you still think I kiss funny?"

She shook her head mutely, her eyes huge.

"Good." Lowering his head slowly toward her, he dropped a few tiny kisses at the corner of her mouth, then whispered, "I've been waiting to kiss you again for a long, long time, Trish. I surprised myself with my patience." He kissed the other corner of her mouth, his tongue flicking out to caress the edge of her lips. "I've been very, very good," he went on huskily. "But now I think I'm going to have to chuck all that nobility and seize the moment."

She hardly heard his words, but her emotions were in complete accord with his, no matter what her warning system was sending out. She'd spent too many days trying to wipe Mason's face from her memory, too many nights tossing and turning with the remembered sensations of his embrace. It was no use trying to deny it. She was hooked on the guy, no matter what.

Forgetting everything else, she lifted her face to his kiss. Her lips parted eagerly beneath his touch, as though her senses remembered how it had been before and were in urgent need of feeling that way again.

Her arms rose and encircled his neck so that she could hold herself more tightly against him. Every fiber of her being was aware of him, wanted him, needed his closeness, his scent, his heat.

His hands seemed huge, covering her back, burning through the cotton cloth of her tank top. Crushed against his chest, her breasts tingled with sensitivity. The crashing of the waves, the scream of the sea gulls, the hot morning sun, the cool ocean breeze, every element seemed to swirl around them as he held her.

Finally he drew back but his arms didn't loosen, and neither did hers. She stared up at him, her lips still quivering, her breath coming in quick, short gasps. She'd never seen anything more beautiful than his face, his eyes, his lips....

"Face it, Trish," he said at last. "We're going to have to start seeing each other."

She pulled away at that, shaking her head, still not thinking clearly, but sticking to the litany. "We can't see each other. We can't."

His gaze darkened. "Do you want to explain to me why that is? I don't think I've ever quite gotten that straight."

What could she tell him? That she didn't dare go out with him because he was such a playboy? She tried to formulate a sentence that told that very truth, but it sounded insulting. She couldn't say it. So instead she said, "Because you're not a ... a serious person."

"Serious?" That brought the humor back to his eyes in a hurry. "I could try getting real serious." He touched her cheek, his eyes darkening. "Just watch me."

And that was exactly what she was afraid of. When he said things like that, she felt her resistance melting like ice cream left out on a hot summer day. Desperately she brought in another excuse. "And anyway, you're part of the problem. You don't want my parents to get back together."

He frowned. "I couldn't care less whether they do or don't."

"But you're helping to keep them apart."

"I'm not doing anything of the sort. I'm just doing my job, the best I know how. What your mother wants to do about your father is no one's business but hers."

She knew he made sense, but emotions didn't care about logic. She avoided his gaze and found something else to use in the brick wall she was trying to construct between them. "You're the one who got angry that day at the Regatta," she said accusingly.

She wasn't sure she should have reminded him. His face hardened as he thought about it. "I had a right to be angry. I don't like being used."

"I wasn't using you."

"Are you going to tell me there was no plot to keep me away from your mother?"

She bit her lip and looked out at the surf. "Well, yes, as a matter of fact, there was. But going down to the marina, going out to the cove . . ." She turned to face him again, her cheeks slightly red, but her eyes clear and candid. "That wasn't part of the plan. I did that because I wanted to. It just happened."

His hand cupped her cheek and he smiled. "Sometimes things that just happen make the best memories," he said softly.

She searched his smoky dark eyes. Did that mean he brought the mental pictures of their time at the cove out to go over in his mind the way she did? Impossible. Surely he had so many other pictures in his vast memory files that the incident between them had faded into nothing.

Which reminded her of Brigitte, the tempting travel agent. They started to walk back across the sand, Mason with his board under one arm and his wet suit under the other, Trish deep in thought. What had ever happened with Brigitte, anyway? Suddenly she had to know.

"So, how did lunch go?" she asked as casually as she was able.

"Lunch?"

"With Brigitte Holloway."

"Oh." His grin flashed in the sunlight. "Fine. Just fine."

The grin hurt, but "fine" meant absolutely nothing. Still she should leave it at that. Not say another word. Do nothing to let him know how important this was to her. Play it safe. Keep quiet.

"So what exactly does 'fine' mean?" She heard the words coming out of her own mouth and she cringed, but it was too late to recall them.

Mason laughed. "Why don't you come right out and say what you mean? You want to know if I had my way with her. Or, more accurately, did she have her way with me? Did I wine and dine her, did I enjoy her womanly charms? Well, I'll tell you, Trish. The answer is—" He threw her a wicked grin. "The answer is, it's none of your business."

Her heart had been pounding with anxiety as she waited for his explanation. Now she wanted to throw something at him. Instead she managed to fake disinterest, turning up her nose and sniffing. "I'm sure I don't care one way or the other."

He nodded and laughed low in his throat. "Right. That's why you advised her to hum her little heart out."

Trish looked up with guilty delight. "Did she do it?"

His eyes were sparkling. "Yup."

They laughed together for a quick moment. "You've got a real cruel streak, don't you?" He shook his head. "I can't believe the stories you'll tell."

They were approaching a big blue van with a huge scene of someone shooting the curl painted on the side. Trish knew it was Howie's. And there he was, waiting in the driver's seat. She stopped just out of Howie's hearing distance and replied to Mason's accusation.

"Well, and how about you? What is this you've told Howie about how I'm staying away from you so that you can concentrate on the business."

He shrugged. "It's true, as far as that goes." His mouth twisted in a bittersweet smile. "Do you think I usually deny myself something I want the way I've been denying myself you?"

She swallowed, unable to speak, heart pounding. Why was he saying these things? Were they just to entice her? He couldn't possibly mean them. Was this just part of his charm? She wished she knew how much she could trust, how much she should disregard.

And then he undercut the tension with a quick laugh and a complete change of mood. "Well, what did you want me to do, tell him you were free as a bird again? Fair game? Easy pickings?"

She blinked. Her heart was spinning with his changeableness. She wished she knew when he was serious and when he was only teasing.

"How did you ever hook up with him, anyway?"

"He's working with us. He just showed up one day and volunteered." Mason smiled at her surprise.

"He's a handy guy to know. He's known you all your life. He's told me all about you—kindergarten—third grade—the senior prom."

"What?"

His evil grin was back, teasing her in a way that drew a smile no matter how hard she tried to suppress it.

"I'm compiling a complete dossier, of course. What do you think? I'm learning the ways of business. Pretty soon I'll know everything about you. And then I can use you to my own purposes."

"Fat chance!" She flashed him a glance she knew was flirtatious, but she couldn't make herself care anymore. She didn't understand him. She wasn't sure she trusted him. But she knew she was overwhelmingly attracted to him. And more and more, that was all that seemed to matter.

He smiled, enjoying her. "Anyway, I don't think you have to worry about Howie anymore."

She looked up in surprise. "Why not?"

"I think he's transferred his allegiance to your sister."

"Shelley?"

"Yes. He moons over her all day long."

"You mean they're all working with you?"

How had this happened? How had everyone gotten caught up in this new business but her? She felt a twinge of jealousy, a flash of resentment that she'd been left out. But that was hardly fair. Everyone had been trying to get her to join in from the beginning. She was the one who'd been holding back.

And another thing—what exactly were they producing at this business? No one had ever told her explicitly. She hadn't wanted to hear. Somehow she had an idea it had something to do with surfing togs.

"When are you going to come down and take a look?" He was serious now, she could see it in his eyes.

That was what it would take to answer all her questions. "I guess I'd better do that right away."

"Today?"

Yes, of course, what was she waiting for? She raised her chin and said firmly, "All right. Today."

He grinned. "Good." He glanced at the van. "Can we give you a ride?"

"No thanks." She was going to need the exercise of a good run just to get over this little encounter. "Well, I'll see you later." She started to walk away, and he called to her.

"Trish."

"Yes?" She looked back.

"Just for your information. Even though I know you're not interested. All that humming gave me a headache and I had to go home early. Alone."

She stared at him, trying not to smile. "You're right," she said coolly. "I'm not interested."

But her grin took over before she'd fully turned away again, and she could hear him chuckling behind her.

Seven

She avoided the issue for almost three hours before she actually got into her car and drove to where her mother's new business was located. The building was long and low, a typically anonymous industrial shell. The sign on the door said WhiteWaterWaves, Inc. With trepidation she pushed open the door and walked in.

At first glance the place seemed almost a replica of her father's. Shelley sat at the receptionist's desk, her textbooks spread out around her, her glasses clinging to the tip of her nose. She was concentrating on her reading and didn't look up right away. That gave Trish a moment to take in the atmosphere, the smells, the sounds. They were all so very familiar. Something stirred in her, a feeling of apprehension. Just what were they making here anyway?

"Hi!" Shelley had seen her. She bounced up out of her chair. "I'm so glad you finally came for a visit.

Come on back and see everything. Mom and Bert are both here, so they can explain it all.''

Was it her imagination, or was Shelley strangely anxious? Trish couldn't imagine why. She followed her into the office. Her mother came toward her with arms outstretched. Bert stood behind her, grinning.

"Trish, baby. Finally you're here. I'm so glad. Come on, you've got to see everything."

She felt a smile stretching her lips and marveled at her own ability to hide what she was feeling. She hadn't realized she could do it so well. Why hadn't she ever explored this talent before? "That's what I came for," she said, and her tone actually sounded light and friendly.

But why was her mother looking at her like that? And when had Bert developed that nervous grin? She followed them to the working area of the plant and as they went, a feeling of unreality was beginning to descend on her.

This smelled like...this looked like...surfboards. It wasn't possible. They couldn't be making surfboards. That would be going into direct competition with her father. That wasn't possible.

But here was the room full of blanks of all shapes and sizes. Her mother was talking but she couldn't focus on her words. Yes, these were blanks all right, the foam interiors that boards were built on. She'd know them anywhere.

She followed the little group to the next room and there were workers applying the fiberglass. There was no doubt. They were making surfboards.

Her mother was still talking, going on and on in an unusually high-pitched voice, but she couldn't understand the words. They passed the sealed, dust-free rooms where the resin was applied and the final coat of paint put on. She'd seen it all a thousand times. But it had always been at her father's. This was just like his place. This was just like his life. What the hell was going on here?

Time suddenly had a weird, dreamlike quality. She had that feeling of being a part of herself, and yet watching herself at the same time, seeing herself put into strange situations that made no sense. She saw herself smile and nod and murmur the proper responses, and it amazed her, because inside something was ripping open and pain was spilling out.

Finally they were back at the office. She looked toward the room with the fiberglass and knew she was going to have to say something. This wasn't right, what they were doing. Laura Becker had deprived her husband of a wife, deprived him of a proper family. Was she also trying to deprive him of a livelihood? Or was it just that she didn't realize what she was doing? Maybe if Trish explained to her....

She swung around in time to see Bert with his arm around her mother's shoulders in a way that told her more eloquently than words ever could have that they were no longer merely friends. Her gaze seemed riveted to his hand, the way the fingers caressed her mother's arm. The shock waves slashed through her like jolts of electricity. For a moment she was afraid she would never breathe again.

And at the same time her mind was working furiously. Of course. How could she have been so blind? This was what it was all about. What a fool she'd been! This had been it from the beginning, hadn't it? There had never been any hope of a reconciliation. Not with Bert around.

Bert had always been around. All her life Bert had been in the background, her father's best friend, his partner, the playboy her mother affectionately disapproved of. Mom and Bert. She felt sick to her stomach.

"Well, I'm quite impressed."

Could that really be her own voice she heard saying those words, calmly, pleasantly, as though nothing were going on. "I had no idea you would be able to get such a big undertaking off the ground so quickly."

They were answering, saying words and phrases that merely buzzed in her ears. And she could see the relief on their faces. For a moment she couldn't think why. Then she realized what it was. They thought she was taking all this very well. They'd expected anger, fireworks, recriminations. And here she was acting as though this whole affair meant no more to her than the weather. If they were relieved at her reaction, she was pretty surprised herself. And not really sure why it was happening.

Bert was displaying some of their finished product, two short boards with needle-noses in the latest hotdogging style. One was hot pink, the other electric blue.

"They're beautiful," Trish heard herself saying with brittle enthusiasm. "I'm sure they'll sell really well. Who's doing your distribution? Where are you planning to market them?"

They were telling her, each stumbling over the other's answers in their excitement over their new project. Trish felt herself smiling, nodding. Suddenly she realized that Mason was in the back of the room watching her. How long had he been there? How long had he been watching her with that dark gaze that saw everything?

And he did see everything. She could see it in his eyes. The others, the people supposedly closest to her, thought everything was all right. They were bubbling with happiness over how well this was going. Only Mason saw right through her fragile facade. His examination cut right into her, saw the pain inside, understood her anguish.

She turned away from him, still smiling, and began to say the words that would let her escape from this hell of a place.

"I'm so glad I came...so happy you're doing so well...this certainly looks exciting...."

She was out the door and walking toward the car, moving like a zombie, praying she would get out of sight before the tears came. And suddenly Mason was beside her, steering her away from her car, leading her to his.

"No," she said weakly. "I've got things I have to do. Let me..."

His hand was a vise on her arm. "I want to talk to you," he said firmly. "Let's go for a ride."

He settled her into the passenger's seat of his midsize sports car and she accepted his direction numbly. She didn't want to talk. She didn't want to do anything but get into her bed and cry her eyes out. But she didn't have the strength to resist him now. He swung into the driver's seat, his large body a vaguely comforting presence to her at the moment. He was such a strong man— so in command of himself and situations. Not that she wanted to lean on him. She didn't want to lean on anyone or anything ever again. If this encounter with reality had taught her anything, it was that she was going to have to stand on her own from now on. She couldn't depend on others. They always let you down.

Mason stole a glance or two at her stiff profile as they drove, but he was as quiet as she was. This was a bit of a test for him, a test he might have set up for himself if only he'd been bright enough to think of it. He knew he had grown in many ways in the last few months. Had he grown enough to be able to give Trish the comfort she deserved?

She sat quietly as they headed for the hills away from the ocean. And she didn't say a word until he'd pulled the car to a stop near a park full of tall, stately oaks.

He switched off the engine and turned toward her. "It's going to be all right, Trish," he said softly. "Everything will work out for the best—and you will survive."

Her insides felt like ashes, but she managed to smile brightly and say, "I don't know what you're talking about." Then he was reaching out and his arms were around her and his hands were in her hair. He was soothing her, giving her the sort of comfort she hadn't had since she was a child with imaginary monsters under the bed and her father had held her to keep away the bogeyman.

She relaxed against him and the tears came, great, wrenching sobs that tore at her throat and hurt her chest. His arms tightened. His voice murmured words that had no meaning, only the sound of comfort, and she clung to him, letting all her sorrow flood out in a torrent that threatened to drown her.

He looked down at her, his feelings intense but confusing. This was the first time he had ever felt such a sense of protectiveness for any woman other than his sister Charity. It was a new feeling. He thought maybe he liked it.

Little by little her grief eased and as she began to reclaim herself, she felt embarrassed to be caught in this situation. She tried to pull away, but he knew she wasn't ready yet, and he wouldn't let her go. He stroked her hair and whispered, "Let it all out, Trish. I'm going to expect you to be strong later on, so get it all out now."

Was this the time to tell her the rest? No. Not yet. Let her get used to the changes a few at a time. Besides, he could think of no logical way to explain it all in one lump. Later was better.

Trish let it all out just as he'd urged. And when she was finished the heavy sadness was still there, but she felt cleaner, better able to deal with her feelings. She straightened and this time he let her go.

"I don't know why I'm crying. I think..." She sniffed and accepted his handkerchief. "I think it's your fault."

"My fault?" His eyes were warm. "How do you figure that?"

She was at a loss to explain but she tried anyway. "I don't know. You hypnotized me or something. I wasn't going to cry at all until you told me to."

They both knew what a load of bunk that was and when she met his eyes, she couldn't help but smile back at the grin she found there.

"Anyway, now that's over. You can take me back to my car and I'll go on about my business."

"I don't think so, Trish. I think we ought to talk it out."

Talk it out? With him? She stared at him and wondered why he would think she would be willing to talk about her darkest fears, her worst pain, with him, a stranger. And then she remembered how he'd understood what she was going through when no one in her family had noticed. How he'd cared when no one else had seemed to have the time. And she knew he was the only one she could talk to. The only one.

"When I was a little girl," she said haltingly, looking down at her fingers twisted together in her lap, "I idolized my father. He was king of the beach. People came from all up the coast to ask his advice, to look at his boards. To watch him surf. He was like a god, with bronze skin and blond hair and a devil-may-care smile. He knew everything. Could do anything. And the rest of us sort of rotated around his light. We lived for him. The whole family."

When she didn't go on, Mason said quietly, "Do you think that's the way it should have been?"

She shrugged, still not looking at him. "That didn't matter. It was the way it was. And we were happy."

He was silent for a moment but she could feel him wanting to say something. Finally he asked, "Do you think everyone was happy?"

She turned and glared at him defensively. "You mean my mother, don't you? You think she was stifled? You think her personality was overwhelmed by the strength of his?" She shook her head with vehemence. "No way. She was always a strong person. She always had her say."

He nodded, not really agreeing with her, but validating her right to her own opinion. "Go on," he said.

"I'm not saying my parents were like Ozzie Nelson and Donna Reed. My mother didn't run around in little lace aprons baking cookies and my father didn't spend his evenings giving us heart-to-heart chats. But there was a strong focus on family. There was a strength of commitment there. A solid foundation. A good life."

"You were lucky you had that. A lot of people don't."

She looked at him, her expression bleak. "But was it all a lie?" she asked him, her voice soft and trembling.

"If they can give it up so easily, was there really anything there? Was I dreaming?"

He looked as though he wanted to take her in his arms again but she couldn't allow that. She didn't want to cry anymore. So she stiffened and he held off and merely said, "If it was real to you then, that's all that matters."

"Is it?" She searched his gaze, wishing she knew for sure. "Then why do I feel so hurt inside?"

He had no words for that one, and instead of speaking he raised his hand to her cheek. She covered his hand with her own, holding his warmth close to her.

"Just don't say to me, 'You're a grown woman. You have your own life. Forget your parents. They don't matter anywmore.'"

"I wouldn't say that."

"But you're thinking it." She tried to smile. "I know it's true. I know it here." She touched her forehead. "But I can't seem to learn it here." Her free hand rested over her heart.

"Tell me one thing," she went on after a moment of silence. "I have to know the truth. My mother and Bert. Are they an item?"

He grimaced. "What do you think?"

It had been obvious. She nodded slowly. "So my father is totally out in the cold. And to add insult to injury, they're going out of their way to produce a product that will directly compete with his." She took a deep breath. "I don't understand. How can they be so cruel?"

His long body moved uncomfortably in the seat. "It's not exactly like that."

"Well, what would you call it? They've taken what he has always been famous for and they're trying to go him one better. What have they done, taken his mailing lists, his specs, his suppliers, his customers—everything he's built all his life? Is this some kind of sick revenge?''

He shook his head, his eyes dark and unreadable. ''It's not like that.''

Her hands were shaking as she brushed hair back out of her eyes. ''Then tell me what it's like.''

He hesitated. Without a response from him she rushed on. ''I feel like this is some kind of fight and I'm going to have to take my father's side because... because he doesn't have anyone else on his side and it's not fair. And I don't want to take his side, because I love my mother....'' Her voice broke and she looked away.

He was silent for a moment, waiting for her to collect her emotions. Maybe he'd been wrong. Maybe it would be best if she went through everything now, all in one day, and got it over with. He turned to her and said quietly, ''If you feel that way, I think there's something we should do.''

She swallowed the lump in her throat and said huskily, ''What?''

''I think we should go see your father. Right now.''

She turned back and stared at him. ''Are you sure you'll be welcome there?''

He nodded, his gaze guarded. ''I've met your father. In fact, he and I have gotten to know each other pretty well over the last few weeks.''

That surprised her. But so what? Just about everything was surprising her today. ''And?''

Mason looked uncomfortable. ''He's all right, Trish. He knows what's going on and he's making adjustments accordingly.''

"I don't understand."

"If you know your father at all, you know he loves the old-fashioned, classic boards. He's been making the newer, jazzier styles for years, just like everyone else, but he doesn't have his heart in it."

"So you're saying he doesn't care if Bert and Mom compete with the short boards, as long as they stay away from his beloved long boards?"

Mason nodded, but Trish remained unconvinced. "I don't know. I find that hard to believe."

"Let's go then. I'll let him tell you himself."

She didn't say anything as Mason started the car and drove it back down out of the hills toward her father's place of business. Instead she went over the revelations of the day and she worried.

What, exactly, should she do? It was all very well to plan to stand by her father and fight for his rights, but she knew enough by now to see what would happen. She could go to her father, tell him how the others were plotting against him, pledge herself to fight at his side— and watch him give her the frown that told her she was beginning to annoy him. Then she'd watch him turn away and go on with his work as though she weren't there. That was what he always did. Hadn't she learned that lesson yet?

If there was to be a fight she would be the only soldier. And for what? To keep her finger in the dike? To try to preserve a crumbling drip castle that was determined to return to beach sand?

She turned and looked at Mason, studied his granite profile, the long, dark eyelashes, the full lips, the straight nose. His hands on the wheel looked strong and competent, the fingers long and tapered, the nails short and neat.

"What do you do when you're upset about something?" she asked him suddenly. "What do you do to help you forget it?"

He glanced at her in surprise. "Me? I don't know." He thought for a moment. "Go skiing, when I'm near snow. Take myself as far away from people as possible and ski until my legs give out."

She nodded slowly. It was the wrong time of year for skiing. But there were other options. "I don't want to go to my father's," she told him impulsively. "Let's go surfing instead."

It was his turn to look surprised. "Do you surf?"

She smiled. "Of course I surf. I'm Tam Becker's daughter. I was shooting the curl before I could read."

He stopped at a red light and turned to look at her. "I'd love to see you out on a board," he said, shaking his head with a glint of appreciative amusement in his eyes. "I'd love to see you hanging on for dear life...."

"Then let's go," she urged, her eyes shining. It seemed something she had to do now that she'd thought of it. And the only person in the world she could imagine doing it with was the man sitting right beside her. "Let's make a day of it. Can you get away for the rest of the afternoon? Let's go and surf our heads off and forget everything else."

He was looking at her intently, studying her, and her enthusiasm began to ebb. He didn't want to go surfing. He'd already gone earlier that morning. Besides, he surely had things to do, places to go. And other people to do things with. He'd already spent more than enough of his time trying to help her. How could she expect any more from him?

The light changed and the car took off and still he hadn't said anything. It was beginning to be embarrassing. She fidgeted in her seat and tried to think of a graceful way to withdraw her invitation. He was pulling up to the parking lot of her apartment building. Well, that proved it. He had been awfully nice, taking her out and comforting her, bucking her up to face the world again. He was probably sick of her by now and just trying to think of a way to tell her so without hurting her feelings.

"Well, say," she said with false cheer as he came to a stop at the curb. "We really should go surfing together sometime. But I'm tired and I'm sure you are, too. So let's take a raincheck on it for today...."

His fingers had curled around her chin before she realized what was happening. She gazed up at him, lost in his smoky dark eyes, rocked by his nearness as he leaned toward her.

"Oh, no you don't, Trish Becker," he said, his voice low and rich. "You promised me surfing. I want to see you in your bikini. I want to see you with sand in your hair." He grinned. "I want to see if you can surf better than I can."

Every inch of her was alive with anticipation and joy. "I...I haven't been surfing for at least six years," she said somewhat inanely, staring up into his limitless gaze.

"Howie says it's like riding a bike," he reminded her.

She laughed. "And Howie knows just about everything there is to know about surfing," she agreed.

For just a moment she thought he was going to kiss her. His eyes softened, deepened. But then his fingers pulled away from her chin and he drew back. She wasn't sure why he'd done that and she wished she had a clue. But it really didn't matter. They were going to spend the day together. Her heart was beating a strong rhythm of excitement in her chest.

"Go on in and get ready," he told her. "I'll go home and get my board and pick you up in half an hour."

With mixed feelings, she watched him drive away. She'd taken a few licks today. She'd been forced to swallow things she hadn't wanted to face. It should be a time of reflection for her, a time to think things through and make adjustments in her life plan. Instead she was heading for the beach with the sexiest man she'd ever met.

"Oh, Trish, you old hedonist, you," she said aloud. And suddenly she was grinning. Why not grab for a bit of gusto? Everybody else seemed to be doing it. Why should she hold herself back? She would go with Mason and she would damn well enjoy herself.

Eight

Mason sat astride his board, his legs in the water, and watched Trish sail toward shore. She was riding a wave as though she had wings, her feet as solid on the board as though she were standing on a sidewalk, her head back, her face transformed. She surfed like an angel. It gave him a glowing feeling just to watch her.

It hadn't been easy to find a beach where surfing was allowed in the afternoon—especially when another requirement was that the waves be uncrowded with other surfers. But Trish had known of a little cove down near the Mexican border and they had headed that way. They had to park just off the highway and hike back a mile, then climb down through jagged rocks and broken railroad ties, walk another hundred yards, then scale a cliff. But it was worth it. The cove had soft, white sand and nice, crisp surf and best of all, they had it all to themselves.

They caught wave after wave and finally dragged their boards up on the sand and collapsed on the blanket Trish had put down when they'd first arrived, panting and laughing and enjoying the warm late afternoon sun on their backs. And then they drowsed.

The sound of the surf pounded like nature's pulse. As his tired muscles began to recover, Mason found himself lying very still watching the woman next to him through half-shut eyes, his mind hovering between dreams and consciousness, his body responding to her presence.

Her hair was drying, turning almost golden as it began to ruffle in the ocean breeze. Her creamy skin was faintly freckled and slightly reddened on her shoulders from the sun. The two-piece suit she wore was hardly a bikini but it was skimpy enough, revealing beautifully-shaped hipbones and a back as smooth as silk. Her face was peaceful, her lashes making long shadows across her cheeks. She was lovely.

Two impulses were at war within him as he came fully awake and studied her. The first was easy to understand. There was a current raging through his body, sending a signal he knew well. "Take her," it said. "She's there for you. She wants you as much as you want her. All you have to do is reach out and run your hand along the curve of her back. She'll be purring like a kitten in no time. She'll be all yours."

In the past he wouldn't have thought twice about a signal like that. In fact he wouldn't have thought at all, but followed it and taken advantage of where it led. But something different was going on this time. Another impulse was getting in the way. It was an urge he didn't understand, an urge that confused him. He knew he'd felt it before, or something very like it, but he couldn't put his finger on exactly what it was.

"Hi." Her eyes were open, suddenly, and she was smiling at him.

"Hi."

Their faces were close, close enough to see the specks of gold in her green eyes, close enough to see the tiny flecks of sand on her earlobe. He felt an odd sort of connection with her that went beyond attraction. He wanted to touch her and yet he held it back, relishing the anticipation, like saving dessert for last.

"That was fun," she said. "I'd forgotten how much I love to surf."

They smiled again, and it was almost too intimate. Suddenly he had to look away, so he half rose and shaded his eyes, looking out at the surf, the white sand beach, the rocky point.

"You know what?" he told her playfully. "This place makes me kind of nervous."

She half rose, too, trying to see what he was looking at. "Why?" She looked up and down the beach, then turned back to grin at him teasingly. "Because you don't have your usual adoring multitudes around you?"

"No. It's not that." He frowned and nodded out toward the sea. "Don't you notice something about this beach? Doesn't it remind you of something?"

She looked again and shook her head. "No. Should it?"

He raised one eyebrow with dramatic significance. "Think Japanese monster movies. Think Gamera and Godzilla emerging from the sea."

She looked again and laughed. "You're right. They always come out on beaches like this." She pretended to shiver. "Too bad we don't have any world-famous scientists along. We're surely doomed."

"Don't worry." He reached out and curled her into the safety of his arm, pulling her close, enjoying the feel of her sun-warmed shoulders, the scent of her sun-baked hair. "I'll protect you."

"My hero." She looked up and smiled and he kissed her, very softly, very tenderly. And then he drew back and examined her face for a long, long time, as though he were trying to find some clue as to why she had the spell over him that she seemed to have.

She stared right back at him, her eyes so wide, so open and innocent. So trusting. He knew that look, knew where it could lead. For once in his life, it scared him.

As if she sensed that, Trish slipped out of his embrace, sitting just a little away, and began talking again, maintaining the teasing tone they'd used before. "I think Gamera and Godzilla are busy in Japan just now," she said with mock earnestness. "In fact, I'll bet there isn't a living monster within miles of here."

He nodded solemnly. "We're all alone. The rest of the world might be gone by now. We might be the only people left on earth."

She made a face. "Then we'd be like Adam and Eve, starting over."

"Yeah." He grinned and wiggled his eyebrows. "Good thing we're engaged."

Her laugh turned into a groan. "This engagement thing has been the biggest pain in the neck. Ever since Howie told everyone at the Regatta, the cards and letters have been pouring in. I've had nothing but offers to cater my rehearsal dinner, offers to cart in an entire orchestra to sing 'Oh Promise Me,' offers to print up

my invitations with invisible ink. I had someone at my
door the other day asking if he could be the one to dye
the shoes for my wedding party. I told him we'd decided to do it barefoot in the park, hippie-style, and he
immediately offered to do the tie-dye banners.''

Mason was frowning, hung up on a previous item.
"Invisible ink?" he repeated doubtfully. "I don't get it.
For people who've already changed their minds?"

"No, silly. You do the invitations in invisible ink and
send them out with a little wax crayon sort of thing.
They have to rub it over the paper for the message to
come out again."

"Ah. Secretly-encoded messages. Sounds like fun."

Their gazes met and it was there again—that feeling
of closeness, of a connection of the spirit, and he felt
the need to make it physical, to extend and explore it.
She was like no woman he'd ever known before—ma-
ture, and yet vulnerable, with depths of emotion and
needs that tugged at him, with surprises that interested
him, with a face that left him breathless. He dropped his
gaze to her tanned shoulders, the V made by her collar-
bone, the soft swell of her breasts in the persimmon-
and-green halter top. Her navel was a dark indentation
in her flat, taut belly. Her legs were long and smooth,
the toenails painted peach. The bottom of her swimsuit
clung to rounded hips and a firm little bottom that
made his stomach knot up. The dull, burning ache that
signaled desire was beginning to throb in him.

He had to look away and hope to quell it. There were
things that had to be done before they could advance to
that stage. Things that had to be said. He knew he was
going to hurt her, and the words stuck in his throat. But
he cared about her. She had to face reality if she were

going to heal from this pain she was suffering. He had to help her do that.

He glanced back and smiled. "You look so great on a surfboard. I'd love to take you up to the mountains. Have you ever skied?"

She shook her head. "Not for years."

"I'd like to see what you could do with a hillside full of fresh powder."

She leaned back and tilted her face to the sun. "I think I'm more of a surfer. I love the sunshine on my back and the hot sand under my feet."

He lay down and looked up at her, shading his eyes against the slanted rays of the setting sun. "Why haven't you ever married?" he asked suddenly.

She looked startled, then relaxed, shrugging. "Anyone besides Howie, you mean?" she said lightly.

He chuckled. "Anyone at all."

It was a subject she didn't care to think about, so she brushed it off. "There really has never been anyone that I felt that strongly about."

He was quiet for a moment, wondering if he should say what was on his mind or leave it. Looking at her again, he steeled himself. He cared too much for her to let her kid herself any longer. "No one ever matched up to your father, huh?" he said softly, then braced himself.

Just as he'd expected she swung on him in shock. "What?"

The outrage in her eyes made him wince, but he knew he would have to see this through now. "It's obvious that you've always hero-worshiped him. Don't you think that's affected your relationship with other men?"

She'd grown so pale so quickly he began to wonder if he'd done the right thing, bringing this up now.

Maybe he should have waited. No. The crisis in her family was happening now. She had to make herself strong enough to survive it.

She was shaking her head as though she could shake away the subject. "No," she said vehemently. "No, that's not it."

He went up on one elbow. "It's pretty hard for a mere mortal man to come up against a myth like Tam Becker," he persisted.

Hot fire flashed in her eyes but she was working hard at controlling herself and when she spoke again, her words were measured. "I've never compared any man I was serious about to my father."

"Right." He paused, then plunged on. "And how many men have you ever been serious about? Name one."

She stared at him blankly and it was obvious she was at a loss to provide one bit of evidence that there had ever been anyone.

"And there won't be any as long as you manage to keep him a myth in your mind. Isn't that why you didn't want to go see him today? Weren't you afraid you might find out something that might start cracking that mythic mantle you've invested him with?"

Trish seemed to wilt before his eyes. Mason moved quickly toward her and pulled her stiff body into his arms.

"Trish, darling," he whispered as he held her close. "I'm not saying this to hurt you. I want you to see that, great as he is, Tam Becker is just a man. When you find out he's human, like all the rest of us, I want you to be able to accept it."

He held her tightly, stroking her back, and waited, but she didn't respond.

"Trish, I know your father. He's a good business-man. A fabulous surfer. And he makes some of the best boards around." He drew back and forced her face up so that she had to look into his eyes, and he smiled. "But listen. All in all, he's not so tough. I can lick him at tennis. And I bet I can ski him off the mountain, too."

And I damn well know a lot more about making a woman happy than he ever knew, he thought, keeping that boast silent.

Still, it was almost as though Trish had thought of that herself. Her trembling lips turned into a sem-blance of a smile, and she began to move in his arms in a way that let him know she was receptive to his com-fort. She lifted her lips to his, and he hesitated only a moment before dropping down to meet them.

Her mouth was hot and he wanted to wrap himself in her heat, so he plunged deep inside, wanting all of her taste, her scent, her feel, to be his and his alone. His mouth possessed hers, taking it like a conquest, and his hands began to move on her back, sliding up and down the smooth expanse, memorizing the feel of her as though he would need it to map the rest of his life with.

She came to him willingly, leaning toward him until the pressure of her slight body pressed him back down on the blanket. She rose above him, and his fingers, almost of their own accord, snagged the closure on her top, flipping it away so that her breasts were freed. He reached up to touch the tips with his tongue, first one, then the other, as she sighed and stretched, luxuriating in the sensation he was creating.

His hands slipped beneath the bottom of her suit and caressed her softness, pulling her into the cradle of his hips. She murmured soft words against the skin of his neck, soft words that drove him crazy with longing to find his way into her soul.

Her body was his right now, his for the taking. But where was she really? Where was her mind? Where were her emotions?

With a growl he turned, moving her onto her back beside him. With desire so intense it burned like a brand within him, he pulled back and looked at her, her copper hair with its golden highlights, her soft, white breasts with their dusky nipples taut and swollen from the tugging of his mouth and the teasing of the ocean breeze, the triangle of soft, auburn hair where her legs met. Her eyes were clouded with her own desire. They looked at him and her arms reached to have him back against her.

He parried her purpose, pushing her arms back and coming down on her body, his hands on either side of her head, holding her precious face.

"We're not going to do this, Trish," he said, his voice husky with his own torment. "We can't."

She stared up at him in bewilderment. "Why not?" she whispered. "I want to." One hand reached up and touched his cheek. "Please, Mason. Make love to me. Make me forget everything else...."

He closed his eyes and swore softly, then looked down at her again, his gaze fierce with concentration on his denial.

"The timing is no good, Trish. Can't you see that? I can't make love to you like this. It isn't right."

What was he saying? Were those words really coming out of his mouth? He could hardly believe it. He hadn't realized he could even think things like that. Self-restraint. It was a whole new concept, but he seemed to be getting the hang of it pretty quickly.

She stared at him for a long moment, not sure whether or not she hated him. She'd never asked a man to make love to her before. And to have him turn her down....

Pushing him away she began to pull herself together, jerking up the swimsuit bottom, pulling back on the halter top, avoiding his eyes with her own. "I'm sorry if I was asking too much of you," she said, her voice shaking. "I didn't realize—"

He stopped her words with a long, hard kiss. "Trish, don't you know how much I care for you?" he demanded, staring at her intently. "I can't treat you like I have all the other women in my life."

"I'm not a virgin, Mason."

"I didn't think you were." He shook his head. The words wouldn't come. How could he explain to her? He'd never before cared about a woman more than he cared about himself. Was that what he was doing here? He wasn't sure. And if he wasn't sure, how could he explain it to her?

Still, he had to try.

"I want you, Trish, but when we make love, I want it to be because you want me, too. Not because you're hurt. Not because you need another warm body close to yours. I want you to want me like I want you. With every fiber of your being, with every ounce of your strength. Like an obsession. Until then, don't ask me to do this."

She gazed at him wide-eyed. Something in his sincere tone finally communicated itself to her. This was special, what he was doing. He was special. She continued dressing slowly, then began to help pack up to leave their private beach. But all the while her mind was busy with this revelation. Mason was a very special man. Probably the most special man she'd ever known.

Nine

It was a typically frantic Monday morning at Paper Roses. Trish was rushing from one customer to the next. The store was full of young mothers with their small children.

She heard the front doorbell chime as yet another person came in, but she didn't look up until she realized that the hush that came over the shop, followed by a rippling murmur, must have been caused by the newcomer. Somehow she didn't even have to see his dark eyes to know it was Mason.

"Hi," he said from across the store, standing there with his hands in the pockets of his corduroy slacks, looking incredibly handsome in his red turtleneck jersey shirt.

All eyes turned from him to her as though watching a ball in a tennis match.

"Hi," she said back, and the room seemed to sway. "I . . . I'm busy."

His eyes were warm, knowing. "I can see that. I just came by to take a look at your place."

He turned and smiled at the crowd. Every young mother in the place smiled back at him, appreciation glistening in their smiles. It wasn't often that a man ventured into this mother and child preserve. And such an attractive man!

"I'll just look around," he said.

There was a new murmur and the crowd parted to make way for him. One bold lady spoke to him, and then another. They were just being helpful, showing him around, explaining the merchandise. But Trish bristled resentfully and wished she had the time to do that herself.

She tried to keep her mind on what she was doing, but it was difficult with Mason around. It had been almost a week since their day surfing. She hadn't heard a word from him since, but she'd thought about almost nothing else. She'd thought about the things he'd said to her. About the things he'd done. And she knew, no matter what else, whether she ever saw him again or not, he'd changed her life forever.

She'd spent the day after their surfing expedition going through the gamut of emotions—anger, sorrow, regret, resignation. Shelley had called to say hello and she'd been blunt.

"Are Mom and Bert planning to get married?"

Shelley had reacted with shocked silence, then a quick, "How should I know? She hasn't said a word to anyone that I know of."

"They are obviously . . . seeing each other."

Shelley had to admit that was true. "They've always been close," she reminded Trish.

"There's 'close,'" Trish answered tartly, "and then there's *close*."

"All right. I'll admit, they seem to be getting...closer. But until she says something, I'm not going to think about it."

"Did she leave Dad in order to be with him?"

Another silence then Shelley said, "You can't blame any one person for what happened, Trish. There's plenty of blame to go around. Enough for Dad, too, no matter how much you try to defend him and pretend that he's perfect." Before Trish could get another word in she added, "I've got to go now. Howie and I are driving up to Laguna for dinner. See you soon."

Trish hung up and stared at her empty room. Howie and Shelley? How very odd. The bookworm and the surfer. But she shrugged and let that go. What stuck in her mind was Shelley's accusation. Was she really that defensive about their father? Had she always been? Why hadn't she ever noticed it before?

That conversation stuck in her mind as she kept an eye on what Mason was doing in her shop. Finally she had a moment free. Wendy, her assistant, took over the cash register and Trish looked around the store for Mason. He was surrounded by helpful women, but when he saw her coming toward him, he immediately detached himself from the group and came to meet her.

She looked up and didn't know whether to let him see how much she loved seeing him here or not. "So you're back," she said evenly, holding back, waiting. "I suppose you came to tell me more things I need to know for my own good, and to make me do more things I need to do for my own good."

He blinked, looking innocent, as though such thoughts had never occurred to him, and shook his head. "Actually, I came to buy some bunny stickers." He showed her the group of them he'd already collected, along with others. "I'm thinking of redecorating my apartment."

Bunny stickers? The corners of her mouth began to twitch and she had to fight to hold back her smile, but somehow she couldn't extinguish her natural streak of sarcasm. "I see. What's your color scheme? Pink and baby blue?"

He was playing it absolutely straight, looking directly into her eyes without a trace of humor in his. "No. It's yellow and pastel green. With little purple flowers."

He couldn't be serious. Could he? She frowned, but he went blithely on, waving the bunnies and other stickers under her nose.

"I was thinking of putting some of these on the walls of my kitchen. Brighten up the place a little."

She looked at him suspiciously. When was he going to admit he was joking? "Great. Butterflies all over your walls. Absolutely. So very masculine."

His eyebrows rose as though he'd caught her in a major faux pas. "Oh-ho. Look who's hung up on gender stereotyping!"

She had the grace to look abashed. "Who, me?"

He sniffed with superiority. "Anyway, I wasn't going to use the butterflies for that. I was thinking more of these little mouse footprints." He held them up for her to see. "Wouldn't they look cute all over my stove?"

She was beginning to wonder if surfing had affected his sanity. "Doing that, you'll guarantee no one will ever stay for dinner again."

"You think so?" He frowned. "Darn. Then how about these spider decals? I could paste them to the bottom of my cereal bowls. No one would see them until they'd drained the last drop of milk. That ought to be good for a laugh or two."

Yes, there it was, a glimmer of amusement in his eyes. That was a relief. At least she was sure he wasn't yet a candidate for the funny farm. "You have a strange sense of humor," she told him. "I don't think you quite understand how to use stickers. Maybe you ought to hold off until you get a feel for it."

"You think so?" He moved closer. "You could teach me all about it in your spare time."

She threw him a quick glance. "I don't have any spare time. In fact, I've got to get back to work. My assistant can't handle this all by herself."

"Too bad." He looked around, pretending helplessness. "Maybe one of these nice ladies would help explain them to me."

There was no shortage of candidates. The crowd soon thinned out but the ones who stayed seemed to have decided to stick around for the duration—at least for the duration of Mason's visit. The children seemed to gravitate toward him naturally, watching what he did, making comments on his selections.

They talked him into getting a plastic box and having it decorated by the resident artist at the decorating table in the back.

"I'm going to keep my tools in it," he told Trish in a low, gravelly voice as he picked out a pale, clear lavender box. "Is that masculine enough for you?"

She pursed her lips but she was teasing and he grinned, knowing it.

He was the star of the show by now, and every child had to have a chance at him. He helped Samantha Knowles pick out stickers for her sticker book, recommending the spiders of course, a recommendation which she scorned. Joel Edwards asked him for a boost so that he could see the porcelain animals on the top shelf, and Jennifer Green insisted that he help her pick out new stationery. He suggested the beige linen with the monkeys on the border, but she opted for the pale pink with a unicorn at one corner.

Trish watched, shaking her head. A lot of the women came up to her and very quietly asked all about Mason, who he was, how she'd met him. She found herself blushing a lot.

At last, business had slowed to the point where she could leave the shop in Wendy's capable hands and go for a walk with Mason. They walked to the corner, bought tacos from a Mexican food stand, and carried them down to the park, sitting on a wooden bench and attempting to eat the messiest food on earth without ruining their clothes.

When they were finished and had thrown away the remnants of their meal and cleaned their hands on the little wet towels provided and sat back to enjoy the sun, Mason turned and looked at her earnestly before he said, "I waited five whole days for you to come looking for me. Five days was all I could take."

She shivered, though she wasn't sure why, and hardly noticed, her mind was so involved with him and what he was saying. "I didn't know there was a time limit."

"Are you angry with me?"

Angry with him? The very concept seemed unimaginable. "Of course not."

He took her hand and stared at it, bending open fingers one by one. "I thought I could wait until you came to me." He looked up into her eyes. "But then I began to worry that you might never come."

"I thought you wanted me to stay away."

"No. God! Whatever gave you that idea?"

"You did. You said that . . ."

His hand tightened on hers. "Forget what I said. Let's start over. Let's start fresh."

She gazed back at him solemnly. There was a depth of emotion in his eyes that startled her, but she wasn't sure how to read it. He was a man who prided himself on superficiality. Wasn't he? Was this all part of his charm? She knew she'd be a fool to take it seriously. Still, she couldn't resist going along for the ride, as long as it lasted.

"All right," she said. "How do we do that?"

For a moment he seemed to be at a loss, but then he had an idea. "We'll go out on a date," he said as though amazed at his own brilliance. "That's it. We'll go out to dinner and dancing. . . ."

She waited for the rest. There was more. It was in his eyes. But he didn't seem ready to state it aloud. Her heart was singing with joy and excitement. She wanted him—in her life, in her heart. She needed his touch, had to have his affection. Love for him rose in her, bringing tears to her eyes.

She knew she was crazy. How could she throw her chances for happiness away on this playboy, this ladies' man? There wasn't a chance in hell that he would stay around long enough to build a life with her. There wasn't even much hope that he would ever want to. But he wanted her right now. He wanted her with a passion that stunned her, and she knew she couldn't go on without him. At least for now.

Suddenly, she smiled. "All right, Mason," she said. "We'll go out on a date."

"Tonight?"

"Tonight."

She knew her fate was sealed, but she didn't care. She loved Mason Ames. That was forever, even if he wouldn't be around to see it himself.

Her hair was getting longer. It curled around her ears now. She'd never wanted long hair before, but now she did. She wanted to feel it sway against her shoulders. She wanted Mason to bury his face in it. She wanted to feel sexy.

Unfortunately, that would have to wait, unless she ran out and bought herself a Dolly Parton wig. She stared at her face in the mirror and tried to imagine what she would look like with one of those blond constructions on her head. Pretty silly.

Sighing, she went back to applying makeup for her date with Mason. She'd bought a new dress to wear. Sea-green with silver threads woven through it, the filmy fabric clung, showing off her breasts, flaring at the hips. It almost made her feel sexy. When she half closed her eyes and whirled before the mirror, she could pretend. But every time she looked at the image fully, she saw her own wide green eyes and freckled nose and all thoughts of "sexy" evaporated.

Was it too late to get plastic surgery done? She glanced at the clock on the wall. Another half hour and he would be here. Probably not enough time.

She felt guilty and excited all at once. Excited because she was pretty sure she was in love. Guilty because she knew she shouldn't be.

She'd thought a lot about what Mason had said about her hero-worship of her father getting in the way of her feelings for more mortal men. And now that he'd made her face it, she couldn't believe she'd been so blind to it all these years. He was right. Absolutely right.

She'd gone to visit her father a few days before. He'd given her a hug and a kiss and then gone right back to sanding and shaping a board he was working on. She'd stayed quiet, watching him, studying the man she thought she knew so well. He was getting older. It hurt to see that. If only she could get him away from work...if only she could pull him out into the larger world... But what was she thinking of? Wasn't that exactly what her mother had tried to do for years? If Laura Becker couldn't do it, why would it work when Trish tried it? All Tam Becker really wanted was to be left alone to do what he loved.

Did he realize what was going on? Did he know that Bert had taken his place at Laura's side? Did he care?

Watching him she realized it wasn't her place to tell him. That sort of thing was between a man and his wife, and even his children had no right to interfere.

But she did bring up business. She asked him directly what he thought about Laura and Bert and Mason going into direct competition with his company.

He shook his head. "No, Trish. I'm getting out of the short board business. The long boards are what I've always loved, made of real wood, shaped just the way the old Hawaiians used to shape them. That's what I'm going to concentrate on. WhiteWaterWaves can make all the short boards they want. It won't bother me." He

smiled at her. "And as for Mason, I think hiring him is
the best thing your mother and Bert did."

To Trish's surprise, her father laughed. "Laura is a
wonderful woman, but you get your business acumen
from me. She's got many talents, but that ain't one of
them. And Bert can shape a board with the best of
them, but he doesn't have that business instinct, either.
Yup, it was a good move for them to bring Mason in."

Her father seemed very serious now. "Mason is what
the surfboard industry has needed for a long time. He's
got fresh ideas for marketing, a background he's
brought over from skiing. He's not as hung up on the
purity of the sport as I am. He'll do things I tried to do
and didn't succeed at. He's going far."

She was glad to know there wasn't going to be a
problem about competition between the companies.
She'd left, shaken, but feeling a bit stronger. In some
ways it was a relief to know that she wasn't expected to
make things right any longer. That she could let things
take their natural course. Because she was out of ideas.
Maybe it was time to learn to accept things as they were.

Mason would arrive any moment now. Had she ever
compared him to her father? She really didn't think she
had. Somehow, with Mason, comparisons seemed ir-
relevant. And then, he was there. Heart beating wildly,
she threw one last glance at her mirror and hurried to let
him in.

It wasn't as though she was unprepared for the vision that greeted her when she opened the door. Still, his
attractiveness never failed to stun her. He looked too
good to be true, especially attired in a beautifully tai-
lored dark suit with a shirt so white it glistened. She
stared for a moment, then pulled herself back, embar-

rassed, feeling as though she'd been caught licking her lips.

But his grin told her he thought she looked pretty good, too. It was wonderful that he never seemed to take anything too seriously. At least, not often.

"Hello, doll," he said out of the corner of his mouth in his best Bogart imitation. "I got your name and number in a fortune cookie. Howz about you and me goin' out to trip the light fantastic?"

She let her chin jut out and did the same with one hip. "I don't know, handsome," she replied, vaguely hoping for a Lauren Bacall tribute, but afraid it was coming out more Mae West. "Can you whistle?"

He demonstrated his capabilities with a long, low wolf whistle that turned her scarlet. She dropped the sultry pose and reached out to pull him inside as doors popped open up and down her hallway.

"Hush!" she begged, laughing at the same time. "That was not kind. I'm going to have to explain you to all my neighbors now. And somehow I don't expect it to be an easy task."

He shrugged, all innocence. "I am but a simple country boy. Tell them I'm your cousin from the Central Valley. My hay truck's taking up three parking spaces in your underground garage, but otherwise, I'm harmless."

"The 'harmless' part is what they won't believe," she told him archly as she reached for her wrap. "You're about as 'harmless' as an alligator in a goldfish bowl."

He looked slightly offended. "Are you calling me reptilian?"

She choked. "Hardly." Her grin was teasing. "I'm just saying you're a flashy dresser."

He frowned, not completely mollified. But she was ready to go, looking up at him expectantly, and he forgot everything else as he turned her in his arms and kissed her softly on the lips.

"People don't usually start dates this way," she murmured as he drew back and looked at her. "They usually save this for the end of the evening."

He brushed her cheek with the backs of his fingers. "And that's exactly what's wrong with the world today," he said, moving toward the door, his arm still around her.

"Not enough kissing?" she asked a bit breathlessly.

"No. Saving things for later that ought to be done right away." He kissed her again and she could tell this was going to be a happy theme for the evening.

They went out into the hallway, and though she closed her door as softly as she could, as they walked down the hallway, two or three doors opened, just a crack. Just enough so that some of her neighbors could check out her escort. They held back the laughter until they reached the end of the hall, but once out of range they let it fly.

They dined at the Sly Fox, sitting out over the bay, watching the boats come in, watching the lights shimmer on the black water. He made her laugh. He made her try expensive wines. He made her feel important, cherished, fun to be with.

They danced at Ricoco's and then on to Whahoo's for the midnight show, and more dancing. They walked along the beach in the moonlight, arm in arm, talking and telling secrets about things they'd done, things they hoped to do.

Trish was moving in a dream, floating on a cloud. She couldn't stop looking at him. He filled her mind and her heart, and everything about him seemed just about perfect. She found herself searching for excuses to touch him, hesitating in doorways so that he would bump gently against her, turning suddenly when she knew he was near, reaching for things just to his other side so that she would have to lean against him.

She'd never behaved like this before in her life, and yet she felt utterly without shame. This was new—this feeling of wanting someone so much. It didn't scare her as much as it astounded her. She hadn't realized she was capable of such a strong longing.

And finally, Mason invited her back to his apartment for a nightcap.

She knew exactly what that meant, what it would mean if she agreed. She'd been so sure, and yet, now that it had been presented to her this way, she felt suddenly hesitant. Maybe it would be better to go on home, this time, and think it over.

"Irish coffee," he coaxed. "With whipped cream and shaved chocolate."

How could she resist?

His apartment wasn't at all the stylish showcase she'd been expecting. The couch was modern, but not imposing, and the coffee table was a slab of polished granite. A Scandinavian hooked rug hung on one wall, and a large redwood sculpture covered most of another. It was a warm room, a comfortable room. Trish searched in vain for evidence of a playboy life-style.

There were some photographs, most of them of two beautiful women. Her heart froze when she first noticed them, and she looked away quickly. But Mason had caught the reaction and he led her straight to them.

"What do you think of these two?" he asked with a mischievous grin as he held up two photos.

"Very pretty," Trish said stiffly. "But then, I suppose all your girlfriends are.. ."

"Girlfriends!" He shook his head as though he were disappointed in her faulty perceptiveness. "These aren't girlfriends. What would I want with pictures of old girlfriends?" He pointed out the one with the friendly smile. "This is my sister, Charity. She's married and runs a restaurant in Mammoth. She's the one who conspired with your mother to get me involved in the surfing business." And then the other, whose look was more dreamy. "My sister, Faith. She's kind of a leftover hippie who hasn't found her way back quite yet."

Sisters. She felt like a fool.

"And this..." He picked up a picture of an older woman, her silver hair pulled back in an elaborate twist, her eyes dark and watchful. "This is my mother."

Trish was oddly fascinated by the elegant face. "She's beautiful."

He shrugged, though his pride was obvious. "She's okay."

"Where does she live?"

He hesitated only a moment, then filled in the blanks. "She's in Hawaii. She's a palm reader."

Trish gaped at him. "A what?"

"A palm reader. 'You will meet a mysterious stranger' and all that." He grinned at her reaction. "Actually, we're very pleased she finally settled down and chose a seminormal career. She and my father used to be con artists. They swindled people all over the South Pacific when I was a kid."

He said the words so matter-of-factly. "With you along?"

"Sure. My sisters and I were part of the act. We lived by our wits. Never a dull moment."

"You make it sound like a Disney movie. The Traveling Ames Show."

He shrugged. "It was like that sometimes. We had a pretty crazy upbringing until we went to live with my aunt in Boston. She taught us what it was to live like proper people." He laughed. "Boring. But ever since then, I must admit, I feel tugged in both directions."

His admission was made so casually, and yet Trish knew there were tragic, as well as comic, aspects to his story. How could children grow up that way, running just one step ahead of the law? And yet that background was probably responsible in good part for the devil-may-care glint in his eye that she found so attractive.

Amazing. And somehow very endearing, too. It explained a lot—like why he might spend his life the way he had—if all he'd been telling her was true, so free of restraints, free to go where he wanted to go, free to be whatever he wanted to be.

He put the pictures down and laughed. "I'm telling you, Trish. I'm considered one of the more stable members of my family." He touched her hair, his eyes glazing over as he leaned near to catch the scent of it. "And getting more stable all the time," he murmured.

A small photo had dropped out from behind one of the pictures and she bent down to pick it up, one hand on his chest for balance. The photo was of Mason holding a laughing baby as though it were the most natural thing in the world for him to do.

"Charity's little boy," he said, taking it from her and flinging it carelessly on the table before turning to take her back in his arms.

"You like children, don't you?" she asked, settling into his warmth.

"They're amusing little monsters," he agreed, looking down into her upraised face. "I was one myself, you
know." He smiled into her eyes. "Some people might
argue I still am."

There were so many things about him that didn't
quite jibe with the playboy image. She knew she was
risking setting off a reaction she might regret, but she
couldn't help herself. There were things she had to
know.

"Do you...do you ever want children of your own?"

Something shifted in his gaze, darkening it, and his
arms loosened around her, and she wished she could
take the words back. "I think I should get married
first," he said lightly. "Isn't that the way it's usually
done?"

It was as if he were slipping away from her and she
didn't know why. His tone was light, but his eyes told
her there was something he was guarding, something
that could come between them if she weren't careful.

She wasn't going to let it happen this time. She wasn't
going to give him a chance to back away from her. She
didn't know, really, why he kept doing it, but she was
ready this time. She would fight it.

She reached toward him, her fingers curling into the
opening of his shirt. "Mason?" She felt shy, hesitant,
but not afraid. The feeling was strong that they both
knew what was right for them, if only they could admit
it to one another.

Mason looked down at her and felt himself melting
inside. He'd never waited so long for a woman he
wanted before. He'd never felt so reluctant once the
moment of truth had come. What was it about her that
brought out this protectiveness in him? He wanted

things to be right for her. He wanted everything to be perfect.

Was this the right time? He knew it was not. There were things between them that should be cleared up first. She didn't know the extent of his involvement. She didn't know his plans. And the only reason she didn't know was because he had been too great a coward to tell her.

What would she do once she realized what he had done, what he was in the process of doing? He wasn't sure. But he knew she would be hurt. He should tell her now, now before she'd committed herself to him so totally they would never be able to walk away from each other again without it tearing them both apart. "Trish . . ." He caught hold of her hand and brought it to his lips to kiss her fingers. "Trish, we have to talk."

"Mason." Her eyes were clear, fearless, and she touched his cheek with her free hand. "You talk too much."

She drew his head down and once she'd captured his mouth with her own, his resistance evaporated like May morning dew. Their kisses had always been magic, and that quality didn't fail her now. His mouth tasted of honeyed brandy and she wanted to drown in it, release herself and float away on the hot, sweet current of his masculine appeal.

There was no more hesitancy in him. His arms came back around her and his mouth moved hungrily on hers, as though he couldn't get enough of her and her need for him. She sighed against him, relief as strong as desire. This was what she had been made for, to love this man. And this time it would happen.

His arms slid down and he was lifting her up, carrying her into his bedroom. She closed her eyes and let her

head fall against him, riding on sensation. There was
nothing more wonderful than love. His hands were
gentle as he laid her down on the soft covers, but his
hands seemed to tremble as he began to unfasten her
dress, his fingers tangling in the crisp fabric. She opened
her eyes then, staring up at him in wonder. How could
he be nervous, a man of such experience? And here she
was, floating, confident, so sure of what she was doing?

There were some doubts, of course. Would he find
her exciting? Would she know what to do to suit his
particular needs? Would she make him feel as good as
others had?

But somehow those fears started to fade, because they
really didn't matter. Something inside told her it would
be all right, that it would work out just fine. She'd been
made for this, just as she'd been made for his kiss.
There would be no problem.

Her dress slid away, making the faintest sound, like
a breeze passing through autumn leaves, and then her
lacy bra was gone, releasing her breasts. Finally his
hands pushed away the silky fabric at her hips, leaving
her unprotected by material barriers.

Being modest didn't even occur to her. She lay back
while he explored her body, touching and testing with
his gentle hands, stroking her nipples erect, flattening
his palm over her soft stomach, smoothing the hair that
refused to lie flat, circling her navel with his warm
tongue, crushing his face between her naked breasts,
sliding his hand along the length of her—until she cried
out with the growing intensity of her response to his
persuasion, and tugged his shirt, wanting him as naked
and free as she was herself.

And soon he was, his long, sleek body shining in the
lamplight. Shy and not completely sure of her recep-

tion, she only touched his bare chest at first. But when her eyes met his she saw the desire smoldering in him, read the urgency there and let her hands move across his warm skin, taking possession. She'd never seen anything so beautiful. She needed to touch him, she needed him close, and her stroking hands began to move more boldly, not thinking, only feeling.

He was so strong, so smooth. He was kissing her mouth, her ears, her neck, her breasts, and she was stroking his back, pressing her body to his, finding him with her hands and guiding him. The sweet ecstasy of anticipation was throbbing in her, making her breath come quickly, making her heart beat like the accompaniment to some wild, sensual song.

"Trish," he murmured huskily near her ear, his voice strained with the strength of his barely leashed passion. "You're so beautiful, I'm afraid to touch you. I'm afraid I'll hurt you."

"Don't be afraid, Mason," she murmured, pulling him down against her, moving with a knowledge sheltered deep within, an instinct that she hadn't known she possessed. She knew deep inside that his control was almost gone, and that she wanted to help free him from it. "You can't hurt me," she murmured, so sure, so in love. "I need you. I need all of you."

Now she was the one who was beginning to tremble with urgency, with a need that grew like the storm inside her.

"Mason!" she cried out, clutching him, her eyes opening wide with surprise and demand.

She moved her hips and he came inside so smoothly that she gasped again with sheer delight, moving with him as though they'd been lovers forever and knew each other's every nuance.

She heard her name. His face was pressed beside hers and he was groaning it again and again. Her fingers moved convulsively on his back, reaching for even more. And she thought she heard his name cried out, then realized only dimly that it was she who had called it.

And then it was over and Trish lay with her eyes shut and her body tightly wrapped around Mason's. She wanted to preserve the moment. Never had she ever felt such soaring joy, as she felt with this man whose body was so close to hers that they might almost be one.

Neither of them spoke. The wonderful magic of their kisses had extended into lovemaking as enchanted as any she could imagine. They lay together very quietly, savoring what had been, savoring all the times they were sure they would have it again.

For there would be other times. Trish knew it had to be. This was more than a passing fling. If Mason didn't realize it yet, she was bound and determined he would do so soon. The ladies' man was about to have the plural erased from his designation.

"Hold me," she whispered dreamily, though he hadn't made any effort to let her go. "Hold me forever."

"Forever," he whispered into her hair, his arms tightening around her.

Ten

—

They made love again an hour later, and then again at the first light of dawn. The magic never diminished. Mason's tenderness never faltered. He seemed to want her as much as she wanted him. Trish was living in a dream, unable to come to grips with such happiness. It seemed too good to be true.

They got up slowly, lazily, even though they both had to get to work. Mason gave her a T-shirt to wear. It barely covered her bottom, revealing quick glimpses of her red panties whenever she bent over, a sight that made him grin happily.

They ate scrambled eggs made by Mason and toast buttered by Trish, and laughed a lot. He loaned her a pair of spandex bicycle shorts to add to the T-shirt, so that she could get home without suffering the indignity of walking down her apartment hallway with everyone noticing she was wearing the same dress home at ten in the morning that she had left in the night before.

They were still laughing as he drove her home and dropped her in front of her building. But the moment she was in through the door, his smile faded and in its place was a look of doom, a look of foreboding. He knew he couldn't put off the reckoning much longer.

He planned to tell her when he met her for lunch later that day, but she was full of stories of what the children had done in the shop that morning, and he let the opportunity slip away. He planned to tell her that evening when they went out to a movie, but they never did leave his apartment. The excitement in what their lovemaking could accomplish was so new, so fascinating, they had to make love again and again just to test it out.

But later that night as she lay sleeping, Mason was still wide-awake for another hour, sitting beside her like a watchful angel, staring into the darkness and wondering how to tell her—wondering about the whole process of needing to tell her. Where had this overriding sense of responsibility come from anyway?

For most of his life he had taken the path of least resistance. He'd never planned his life. It had merely happened. True, it had been a selfish, useless existence. But it had been his.

Now he hardly recognized that old Mason Ames. He was a different person with different needs. He was learning how to work for what he wanted. And he was also learning that doing that wasn't always easy. There was a price to be paid.

He looked down at Trish and felt a fullness of emotion that was new to him. Was this what he wanted? Was this something he wanted to trade away his freedom for? The questions were new and it would take time to find the answers.

In the morning Trish woke and stretched, feeling deliciously lazy, then turned and found Mason awake and up on one elbow, watching her. His haggard look alarmed her.

"What is it?" she asked, reaching out for him. "Didn't you sleep?"

He grabbed her wrist before she'd touched him, holding her back. "Wait a minute, Trish. I have to talk to you."

She felt as if she'd been dashed with cold water. A terrible dread began to flicker in her. She pulled back her hands as though she were folding in upon herself. She'd known this was too good to be true. Now he would tell her why this wouldn't work. She could see it in his eyes.

"What is it?" she asked in a small voice, though the last thing she wanted was to know.

His dark face was troubled. She wanted to comfort him but she could see he didn't want that. Not right now. Not from her. He was going to tell her things she wasn't going to like. She held her breath as though that act could hold back his words.

"Trish." He winced before he went on, and in that moment the harsh sound of the telephone sent jolts through both of them, stopping them cold. They turned and stared at the phone, and then Trish reached out to grab the receiver as though it were a lifeline saving her from drowning.

"Hello?"

"Trish?" It was Howie's twanging voice. "What are you doing there?"

"My laundry, what do you think?" She bit her lip, regretting her sharp tone. "Did you want to speak to Mason?"

Howie's sigh rang in the receiver like wind through a tunnel. "No, I guess not," he said sadly. "I was going to ask Mason if he wanted to bring his board down and catch some big ones, but . . ."

She put her hand over the mouthpiece. "Howie says the waves are great," she paraphrased to Mason with a winning smile. "Let's meet him. We can get in an hour of surfing before we go to work. What do you say?"

He hesitated, but his worried look couldn't withstand the charm of her eagerness. His face broke into amused affection and he nodded. "Sure," he said. "Why not?" Rising from the bed, he headed for the bathroom.

She watched him, knowing she was being a coward. She knew he had something to tell her, but she also knew instinctively she didn't want to hear it. This would put it off a little while more. And right now she felt as though every moment of happiness was stolen from the gods.

"It's all set, Howie," she said a bit breathlessly. "We'll meet you at the pier."

The days flew by and the problem seemed to recede. Mason didn't try to bring it up again and Trish could almost forget that it was lurking in the background. They enjoyed every minute together, and when they lay in each other's arms, she couldn't imagine how anything could ever tear them apart.

They took long walks on the beach and danced under the stars and went to the zoo to laugh at the animals. She fed him barbecued hamburgers and he made her a monster hot-fudge sundae and they read the Sunday funnies lying side by side on the floor of his apartment. And then they went to a surfing contest in Huntington Beach.

The beach was lined with the usual mythical California girls in bikinis, but Mason only had eyes for the competitors, Trish was pleased to note. He was fascinated by the contest, completely captivated by the drama of the fierce competition and the romance of the setting. He fired questions and she tried to answer, though it was tough when he had a new question ready even before the old one had been fully dealt with.

They paced up and down the beach, arm in arm. She told him everything she knew and he soaked it up like a sponge.

"I love this," he said at last, his arm sweeping wide to include the entire scene. "This is great."

That warmed her because it was her life he was talking about, the life she'd always known. If he loved it maybe he loved her a little, too. Just a little. That was all she asked right now.

She introduced him to surfers she knew, mostly older ones, because she hadn't been around the surfing scene for years and didn't really know most of the younger ones. But as they were pushing their way through the crowd toward the judging stand, the hand that came out and grabbed Mason by the shoulder belonged to one of the stellar stars of surfing, Shaun Gibbons, a man she had never met.

"Mason Ames! Hey, buddy, what brings you down to the beach? Did all the snow melt up there on your mountains?"

Shaun and Mason clapped each other on the back and threw good-natured insults back and forth. Trish interpreted what was said to mean they'd met before, mostly on the ski slopes, and were good friends. A large, blond, suntanned bear of a man, Shaun invited them back to the tent for a cold drink and a few more moments of memories and kidding between the two men.

Trish enjoyed watching the two of them interact. It was nice seeing how respected Mason was by people who knew him as a skier. But suddenly the conversation took a turn that chilled her.

"Hey, man," Shaun was saying, throwing his big arms wide. "You ought to try surfing. For real, I mean. Get yourself up to speed and join us on the tour."

Mason laughed, his white teeth gleaming against his dark skin. "I'm not in your class, Shaun. Never will be."

Shaun shook his shaggy head. "Are you kidding, someone who can ski the way you can? It would only be a matter of time and training before you got good enough to play with the big boys."

Mason looked pleased but skeptical. "I'm afraid I'm a little long in the tooth for that."

"Who knows? The sport is always changing. And hey, listen, there's a place for you out there on the pro tour." Shaun's eyes lit up as though he'd had a sudden inspiration. "It's your kind of life, man. Believe me." He grinned knowingly. "Listen. You know a lot about managing. I'm in the market for a new manager right now. I could use someone with your kind of moxie."

Trish's every instinct for survival was quivering. She looked at Mason and right away she could tell he was interested. No, more than interested. Call it thrilled.

No, no, no, she wanted to cry out. No, don't ask him. But Shaun did, making a formal offer that included a shocking amount of money. She watched Mason shake his head, but she saw the regret in his eyes. He was tempted. Lord, he was so tempted!

What had stopped him from jumping at the offer, she wondered later as they wandered farther down the beach, alone again, arm in arm. Had he really decided the work-a-day world was where his future lay? Had it been because he loved his job? Or could it have had anything to do with her?

He began to sing softly in her ear, a Hawaiian song he must have learned when he was young. She remembered what he had told her about his childhood, the South Pacific setting, running from one island to another, excitement at every turn. Did he still long for that? She pressed herself more tightly against him as he sang, and when he tilted her face up for his kiss, she responded hungrily.

"What is it?" he asked her, his hand in her hair, his eyes searching hers. "Is something wrong?"

She shook her head mutely, not trusting her voice. *I love you,* she wanted to say. *I love you and I want you to stay with me. Forever. Please, please promise you'll stay.* But those words didn't fit into the rules of the game they were playing, and if she used them she knew she might be disqualified from further play. So she kept quiet, smiling at him rather tremulously, and he kissed her again and whispered, "Let's go home. Okay?"

Home. That wonderful, comforting word.

"Yes," she whispered back. "Let's."

"It could work," she told herself aloud as she floated in a lovely bubble bath the next morning. She was alone in her apartment getting ready to go to Paper Roses within the hour, but needing time to think right now.

"It could work," she insisted to the empty room, as though someone had contradicted her earlier declaration. "Mason might be one of those men who, having sowed his wild oats, is ready to settle down and start a family."

Marriage. Funny how she'd never noticed before, but the word had a warm, happy sound. Marriage. It made her think of a cheery fire on a country hearth, children playing on a rolling green lawn, a golden wedding band with names engraved inside. Why on earth had she been so concerned about her parents' marriage, when all the time she should have been considering one of her own?

She loved Mason with all her heart, loved him so strongly it made her smile to think of his face, made her close her eyes to think of his voice, made her gasp to think of his body. She loved the way he moved, the way he raised one eyebrow when he was teasing her, the way his hand reached out protectively when they walked together. She could no longer imagine life without him. He was hers. She was his.

She sighed and reached for the soap. "It could work," she told the bar sternly. "I know it could."

She finished her bath and dressed slowly, relishing her new-found certainty. This thing was going to work out. All she needed was a little patience, and then Mason would come to that conclusion on his own. She glowed with happiness. It was going to work.

If she'd been a few minutes quicker, she would have missed her sister's visit, but as it was, her hand was on the doorknob when the knock came and the next thing she knew, Shelley was flying into the room in full fury.

"I knew he was trouble the minute I saw him. Didn't I tell you at the time? Do you remember when I called you and told you—"

Trish kept foreboding at bay and cried, "Shelley, will you calm down and tell me what this is about?"

Shelley shook her head, her eyes gleaming with anger. "He quit. That's what this is about."

Trish was still baffled and hanging on to shreds of hope. "Who quit?"

Shelley took a deep breath and spit out, "Mason Ames, that's who. He couldn't take being told what to do by a woman, I guess. So he quit." She flounced down onto a chair. "We should have known it would happen sooner or later. It wasn't as though he'd ever had a steady job before."

"Shelley." Trish felt sick, but she had to get this straight before she let her emotions overwhelm her. She sank down on her knees beside where her sister sat and took her hands in her own. "Shelley, please. Start from the beginning and tell me exactly what happened."

Shelley threw her head back dramatically. "Mason came into work this morning at eight, as he always does, and Mom called him into her office to tell him she disagreed with some order he had made or something, and the next thing I knew, he was saying, 'This isn't going to work, Laura. I told you before that I didn't think we were turning out to be a compatible working team. And I guess this proves it. I'd better go clear out my office.'"

"He quit." Trish closed her eyes and shuddered. "Oh, my God. He quit."

"Can you believe it? And after all Mom has done for him, too. You'd think the man would have more loyalty. Even Howie was shocked."

"Yes." Trish rose slowly, her eyes on some distant horizon. He had quit. He had turned his back on the work-a-day world after all. The dream was over.

"I don't know if Mom can carry on without him."

Trish blinked at her distractedly. "She still has Bert," she murmured.

"Oh, Bert." Shelley threw up her hands in exasperation. "You know how he is. Lots of fun, but not much on the ball when it comes to business. No, Mason has been carrying that company." She shook her head. "I only hope Mom can take over and do it alone."

A sound made them both turn to find Mason standing in the doorway where Shelley had left the door ajar.

"You!" Shelley accused, rising as though to confront him. "Traitor!"

"Shelley." Trish put a hand on her arm to restrain her. An icy calm had settled over her. "Please go now. I want to talk to Mason alone."

Her sister obliged but not without another scathing glare as she passed Mason and left. Trish hardly noticed. She was staring at Mason, trying to read his impassive face for hopeful signs. So far, she could find nary a one.

"You heard," he said at last.

"I heard," she answered softly. "But I don't understand." She raised her hand in a helpless gesture. "Why?"

He turned from her and walked toward the sliding glass door that led to the balcony, staring out at the ocean beyond. "It's been coming for a long time, Trish. I've been trying to think of a way to tell you."

She came up behind him, wanting to touch him, not daring to. There was a feeling of inevitability to what was happening here. And yet, she couldn't give up without a fight. She licked her lips and said quickly, "But I thought you were so happy with the work. I thought you were excited about it."

He turned to face her, his eyes troubled. "I was. I am. The work is great, and I'm good at it." He shrugged, searching for words, starting to reach for her, and then pulling back his hand. "I ... Your mother and I have our disagreements. We had one today. I got a great chance to begin marketing our boards in Florida. She doesn't think we're ready for that. She wants to take it slow, take it easy." There was a grimace on his handsome face. "Be *sure* first." He shook his head. "I don't have time for that. I don't have time for the hassles."

Trish felt a trembling inside. She clenched her hands together to hide it from him. "Can't you go back and talk it out with her? I'm sure—"

He made an impatient gesture, shaking his head. "There's no use in beating a dead horse. This isn't me, this nine-to-five scene. I was never comfortable with it even right from the start."

Yes, she'd seen that. And hoped against hope that he would change. She nodded, turning away, not wanting to hear any more. He wasn't meant to settle down. That was all there was to it. Of course she understood. He didn't have to try to explain.

He turned abruptly and shrugged, his voice rougher, harder. "I've tried to warn you not to expect too much from me. I can only do what I can do, Trish. You can't ask me to make myself over into something I'm not."

Was that what she'd been doing? Asking him to conform to the image she wanted him to reflect? Of course it was. And yet, how could anybody become different? She was what she was, as well. She couldn't change any more than he could. She wanted order and stability and security. He wanted freedom.

"You're running away," she said dully, feeling sick. "Instead of seeing things through." Something was dying here, and she had no idea what to do to revive it.

His laugh was harsh and humorless. "If you say so, Trish."

She shrugged helplessly. "What...what are your plans?" she asked, trying hard to keep her voice from trembling.

"Plans?" He said the word as though it were foreign to him.

"Plans. Those things most adults make before they move on. An outline for the future." Her tone wasn't sarcastic, though her words were ready-made weapons. "If you're not going to work for my mother any longer, what are you going to do? Go back to being a ski instructor?"

He stared at her, frowning slightly. "I don't know, Trish. Maybe I'll take Shaun up on his offer and follow the surfing tour." He smiled suddenly and reached for her, his hands on her shoulders.

"What about it, Trish? Would you come with me to Australia and sit on the beach with me?"

A wave of sick remorse swept over her. She knew what she ought to say. If she really wanted this man, she ought to say "Yes, Mason, I'll follow you anywhere. Anywhere and everywhere. I'll change my life for you." After all, wasn't she expecting him to change his for her?

But when the challenge was presented, she knew it wouldn't work. She was too old, too sure of what she wanted to totally remold herself for someone else, no matter how much she loved him. There were things she needed from life. Stability. Certainty. Control. She couldn't give them up.

"Tell the truth, Trish," he was saying cannily. "Don't kid yourself."

She couldn't say a word. To say yes, she would follow him, would be a lie. To say no would be to say goodbye. The words stuck in her throat, along with a lump made by the tears that were gathering in her eyes.

Mason stared at her for a long moment, recognizing the significance of her silence. A bittersweet smile hovered on his lips. "I guess I know my answer," he said softly. Reaching up, he touched her cheek. "Goodbye, Trish," he added, and then he was turning away, striding for the doorway, and out of her life.

Trish spent the rest of the day in quiet agony. She refused to use this pain as an excuse to get out of her daily routine. She went to work and snapped at Wendy, then hid in the back doing paperwork so that she wouldn't do the same to her customers. And it was all a sham to keep from thinking. But, of course, her mind couldn't let go of the thing anyway.

What had she done? Had she really let the man she loved walk away without even trying to hold him? Was she crazy? Was she really so weak, so helpless, that she could think of nothing to do to keep him with her?

It made her furious to think about, and every time she got furious, she got up and began to pace around the office, until Wendy finally came in to see what all the thumping was about.

"I'm doing laps," Trish grumped at the poor woman. "Haven't you heard? Exercise is good for you."

Wendy beat a hasty retreat, and Trish went after her to apologize. She decided to go outside, and then she was suddenly walking along the beach, hoping the sound of the surf would drown out her sorrow and anger.

The anger began directed at Mason for disappointing her, and ended up being directed at herself for being unable to cope with what he had done. After all she knew what he was like when she fell in love with him. If she'd wanted a dull, stable man, she certainly had had plenty of other opportunities to fall in love with one of them. It had been Mason with his laughing eyes and his devil-may-care grin who had captured her heart. He was only acting true to type. And now she couldn't deal with it.

Suddenly she needed to see her mother. Mothers had the answers, didn't they? Resolutely she went back to her car and drove to her mother's new place of business.

There was no one at the reception desk. She frowned, worrying. Her mother and Bert were really going to have to tighten up their business practices. She walked through the lobby and back into the workshop area. There was no one around. But through the textured glass of the office she could see that someone was inside. She sighed, then pushed onward, shoving open the door and calling, "Mom?"

The figure turned around, but it was Bert's broad face that greeted her.

"Hi, Trish," he said cheerfully. "Your mother went out for a few minutes. She ought to be back soon. You want to come on in and wait?"

Trish hesitated only a moment. Bert had always been like an uncle to her. There was no reason to begin treating him like he had a contagious disease.

"Sure," she said as she sat down. "So, how's business?"

"Fine." He beamed. "It's great getting back in the swing of things again. Laura is a great lady, you know. I don't know what I'd do without her. She saw me down in the dumps and she got this whole idea going so that I could get back up and feel better. She's a great lady, yes she is."

His obvious affection for her mother couldn't help but warm her a bit. Maybe this was just what her mother needed after all those years of being half ignored by Tam Becker. A little indulging, a little pampering, a bit of coddling and attention—of course she deserved it all. Who was Trish to demand she deny herself a bit of happiness?

And then her mother breezed into the office, chattering merrily as she led Trish away from Bert's office and into her own.

"I'm glad you came, Trish," she said at last when they were alone and seated across from one another. "I've been wanting to talk to you. There are things you should know."

Trish looked up quickly, half with guilt, half with foreboding. So far today the things people had wanted to tell her had not been things she'd wanted to hear.

"I know you've been upset about the way matters stand between your father and me. And that you've noticed how close Bert and I have become. And I know that's bothered you, too."

Trish nodded, unable to deny what was obvious.

Her mother leaned forward and reached for her hand. "Did you know that Bert and I were sweethearts long before your father ever came into the picture?"

No, she hadn't known that, and the knowledge shocked her. She shook her head, her eyes huge and watchful.

"Well, we were. Those days were so long ago, it almost seems like another age. But it was a lot like those beach party movies they used to make, only not quite so silly. We lived at the beach. We bodysurfed, mostly, and built huge camp fires and roasted hot dogs and danced in the sand. Bert and I ran around with the same crowd. We were going to get married."

"I know you've heard the story before of how your father arrived carrying a big long board. He didn't look to the right or the left. Just headed straight out into the surf. And when he stood up on the board and rode a wave in, we all thought we'd died and gone to heaven. It was like something out of a fantasy novel. We all went wild for him and his surfing."

She could see him doing exactly that, just that way, his self-contained arrogance flying like a flag.

"Bert was wild in those days. You never knew what he would do from one day to the next. But Tam Becker—he was solid as a rock. When he asked me to marry him, I had to make a choice. I chose something I was sure of and let Bert slip away."

"So all these years..." Trish shivered, thinking of all the emotion lurking behind the smiles she'd grown up with. How could she have been so unaware? It seemed impossible. And yet it must have been true. Look at the results they were all reaping today.

"Bert and I never did anything, or even said anything to one another, that we couldn't have said in front of your father. Not until this last time I left, when I had really decided it was over."

She believed Laura implicitly. "Are you planning to marry him?"

Laura's eyes were shining. "What do you think?"

Funny how the knowledge didn't hurt her any longer. It was, after all, her mother's life.

"Trish," Laura said as she showed her out. "I just want to say one more thing to you." She took her daughter's face in her hands and smiled at her. "Follow your heart, my darling. Whatever you do, make sure you follow your heart."

Trish left even more confused than she had been when she'd arrived. There was too much to digest. She went back to the beach and walked for hours, her mind turning over and over the things her mother had told her, adjusting history as she ate up the miles.

When she ran out of beach she hit the sidewalks, and suddenly she found herself standing in front of her father's business. She hesitated, staring at the building she knew so well. Taking a deep breath, she went to the door. Maybe it was time to get his side.

Grace, the receptionist, waved her right in as she always did. Her father was seated behind his desk, paperwork spread out in front of him, glasses pushed up on his forehead.

"Hi, Trish," he said with a smile when he looked up and saw her standing before him. "What's got you all riled up this time?"

She bit her lip, not sure what to say. "I . . . Mason Ames . . ."

Her father grinned and interjected, "Well good. It's about time some man got under your skin. You going to marry him?"

She flushed and drew back. "I'm not talking about my romance, Daddy. I'm talking about yours."

He looked surprised. "Romance? I don't have any romance."

She bit her lip. "Please talk to me, Daddy. I have to know the truth."

He stared at her for a long moment, then nodded slowly. "Your mom and I—the marriage is over."

"Yes." She felt tears prickling but she took a deep breath and refused to give way to them. The mourning period on the marriage of Tam and Laura Becker was officially over. "I understand that."

"Then you've given up the matchmaking activities?"

"Yes."

"That's a relief. Anyway, she's gone back to Bert. That's where she belongs."

"I know that must hurt you."

"No, Trish, you don't know that at all. Because it doesn't." He frowned. The effort it took him to talk about this was obvious. "I'm a loner, Trish. I probably never should have married at all. But we did have some good years, and we did get two beautiful daughters out of it. And for that, I would do it all again."

Had it really been worth it? she wondered. Why had they ever married in the first place, if it wasn't meant to be? "Daddy? Why did you marry Mom?"

He stared at her as though she'd asked something utterly ridiculous. "I married your mother because I loved her. Loved her madly. Couldn't live without her."

"Oh."

"We grew apart. It was nobody's fault, Trish. It just happened."

It just happened. Trish stood, ready to leave. "I love you, Daddy," she said suddenly, rushing into his arms.

He held her awkwardly, patting her back. "I love you, too, honey," he muttered. "You know that."

She knew it, but it never hurt to hear it again. Walking slowly from the building, she began to realize something else. Life moved on. Change was unavoidable. But people made their own happiness. The future resided inside her. She could do with it what she wanted. Her parents had both reached out and taken hold of their lives. Why couldn't she do the same?

Eleven

She spent a sleepless night and woke from a fitful doze to find a morning fog had rolled in, the first of the fall. The gray mist was a perfect complement to her gray mood. She fixed herself some very strong coffee and sat in her window seat to watch the fog send out its tendrils, filling the area with an impenetrable shroud of cool moisture.

The unopened mail from the day before caught her eye, and she reached for a large manila envelope included with it. Ripping it open she found four prints of herself and Mason kissing that spring day at the Regatta. The note attached said, "Found some extras of these and thought you might like them."

She stared at the photos. They were a handsome couple, these two on the glossy paper. Made for each other. The magic was there in their faces. She could feel it again, like the remembered refrain from a song. Ma-

son. Lord, but she loved the man! She longed for him.
All the other little things that had once filled her life
seemed useless and empty. Without Mason her spark
was gone.

She looked around groggily, as though emerging
from a deep sleep. What was the matter with her? What
had she been thinking of all this time? Life without
Mason would never satisfy her. Was she crazy? She
would rather have Mason with all his wanderlust than
anyone else in the world. There was nothing here for
her, nothing at all, if he weren't around to share in it.

Once that was settled her way seemed so clear. She
dressed quickly in jeans and a long-john shirt, then
raced down to the parking garage to her car.

It took only minutes to get to his apartment. She
raced up the steps and pounded on his door, ringing the
bell at the same time. Again. And then came the realization that there was no answer. No one was home.

"Are you looking for Mason Ames?" asked a woman
passing by on her way to another apartment. "I saw
him walking toward the beach with his surfboard."

The beach. Of course. She thanked the woman, ran
to her car. How would he receive her? She wasn't sure.
Still, she had to see if there was a chance to get back into
his heart.

Mason stared out through a clearing in the fog and
watched dolphins surging one by one out of the gray
ocean, their silhouettes against the silvery sky.

There was sand in his hair and wetsuit. Still, sitting on
the beach, his board beside him, the waves breaking
before him, he had to sigh with contentment. This was
the life. Pity those poor slobs in their three-piece suits
marching off to work in cold, concrete buildings all over

town. He'd escaped from the horror of that daily drudgery, never to go back. He would surf until he was sick of it, and then he would return to the mountains.

He leaned back and tried to visualize himself on the snowy slopes. The picture wasn't coming clear. Frowning, he tried harder. Step by step, he took himself through a typical day at Mammoth—the breakfast in the chalet, the thrilling rides down the runs, the evening before the fire and dinner at Harwood's Glen. That reminded him. He wanted to take Trish there. She had to try those steaks the way Harwood grilled them. And his special steak sauce...

Mason's hands clenched spasmodically and he cursed aloud. No, dammit! He wasn't going to think about Trish any more. She was out of his life, just as all the other women he'd ever known were out of his life. It was over. Over.

But why couldn't he get her out of his head?

He would think about something else—his apartment and how he was going to get out of the lease, the new car he wanted to buy if he had any money left after he'd paid off all his bills and moved his things back to the mountains.

That reminded him. The resin supplier for White-WaterWaves was due his check for the last shipment. He'd had the secretary file the invoice, but when he'd asked her for it, she hadn't been able to find it. He'd meant to do something about that, but then he'd quit. Would Laura remember? Probably not. Maybe he should just go by and...

He sat very still, stunned. What was the matter with him? He wanted to go back to his desk at White-WaterWaves and get back to work. Was this crazy?

He missed work, and even more, he missed Trish. Things had gotten so bad, he couldn't even imagine life without her. She was in his dreams, in his heart. He might as well admit it. He wasn't going to get over her easily. He wanted her back, wanted to feel the silkiness of her hair, the warm excitement of her kiss. He just wanted her nearby, wanted her there to tell things to, to smile at him, to react to his jokes.

He said it aloud. "I'm in love."

A passing surfer looked at him strangely, but he didn't even notice.

"I'm in love," he repeated, feeling his face light up with wonder. It broke over him like a wave, this new realization. He could go back to his old life, but he would never be happy now. Not without Trish. He needed her more than he needed freedom. He needed her more than he'd ever needed anything in his life.

He could go back to the company. He knew he'd been running away, just as Trish had accused him of doing. He'd come down here to San Diego to change his life, and he was now in the process of blowing it and ending up worse than before he'd come. What a self-indulgent idiot he was. This had to stop.

Excitement welled in him. He would go to Trish and spill it all out and somehow convince her to take him back, give her another chance. And then he would go to Laura and work something out.

He rose and looked down at the board in the sand, then out at the swells in the ocean. One more ride. He would take one last ride, a symbolic farewell to the old Mason. And then he would get on with his life. Grinning, he took up the board and began to run toward the surf.

It was only a few blocks to the beach from Mason's apartment, but Trish felt as if she'd been driving forever. She could hardly wait to see him again and talk to him. A siren blared through the mist and she saw an ambulance race by. It was the paramedics, coming from the beach.

The beach. Suddenly it sank in. There wasn't anything out here on the point but the beach. And who would be out there on a morning like this but surfers?

Fear rose in her. She was shaking, but drove on steadily toward the beach. She pulled into a parking space close to the sand and jumped out to run toward the small knot of people she saw milling a few yards away.

"What happened?" she demanded, fear making her voice harsh. "Who got hurt?"

One of the young men turned and filled her in. "I don't know. Some surfer got hurt. Board hit him or something. He was out cold. They had to pump air back in him."

Mason. Oh Lord, could it be him? He wasn't very experienced at surfing, and he was out here all alone. "Is he all right?"

"Who knows? He looked pretty blue. Some guy was giving him artificial respiration like there was no tomorrow and then the paramedics came."

"What did he look like?"

"I don't know. He was all wet, you know? He had on a blue springsuit. There's his board."

Trish whirled and stared down at the short board painted in stripes of day-glo pink. Mason's board. Her heart sank and her knees almost let go.

"Where?" she gasped, turning beseechingly toward the man. "What hospital?"

"Balboa Central, I guess." He called after her as she began to run for her car. "Hey, I'll give his board to the lifeguard to hold for him, okay?" Trish didn't answer.

She was back in her car and trying to maneuver it although her hands seemed to have turned into clubs. Her heart was beating so hard in her throat, she had to force air around it to breathe. Back in traffic she zipped in and out of the lanes, muttering little prayers as she went. He had to be all right. What would she do if he were badly hurt?

She parked in the emergency entry and ran in through the huge glass doors, skidding to a stop before the desk. "Mason Ames," she cried breathlessly. "Where have they taken him?"

"Mason Ames?" The nurse frowned, checking her list. "I don't have any Mason Ames listed here."

"The surfer. He was just brought in. He was hit by a board."

"Oh, the surfer? They took him in that way, but listen, miss, you can't—"

Trish was in no mood to hear what she could or could not do. She dashed in through the gurneys and stacks of equipment and found the row of little cubicles set apart by screens. She grabbed an orderly and asked, "Mason Ames? Where have you taken him?"

From behind her came a familiar voice. "I'm right here, Trish. What's the matter?"

She whirled and there he was, standing straight and tall and not at all injured, his hair plastered against his head from the salt water, his body encased in his short wetsuit.

"Mason?" She came up and touched him as though she was afraid he was merely an apparition. "Are you all right?"

"I'm fine. It wasn't me who was hurt. It was some young kid. I just helped bring him in."

"Oh, my God." She clung to him, tears welling in her eyes. "Mason, I was so scared." The lump in her throat hindered further speech and she pressed herself tightly against him sobbing quietly.

He held her, his arms gentle, his face in her hair. "Trish, Trish, you feel so good."

She looked up, her face tearstained. "You're really all right? Nothing broken?"

His crooked smile warmed her. "Only the heart," he told her sadly. "It got broken a few days ago when you turned your back on me. Otherwise, I'm okay."

The heart. How could he joke at a time like this? But when she looked into his eyes, she could see the joke was only a way to cover the depth of his emotions, for it was all there, burning in his eyes. There was no room in her any longer for doubts. Maybe Mason had always been a ladies' man. That didn't matter any longer. He was her man now.

"Oh, Mason," she said shakily. "Let's go home."

She had no idea why home was suddenly his apartment, but it was. They drove back in her car and he told her how he had seen the boy go down, how his board had hit him and now he'd disappeared under the surface.

"I had to dive a few times, but I finally got hold of him with one hand and pulled harder than I've ever pulled anything in my life. I got him up on the sand and tried CPR. I think it helped. He was breathing when the paramedics arrived. They think he'll be okay."

"You saved his life."

"Maybe. But so did the paramedics. And so would anyone else in the same situation."

She didn't want to hear that. He was a hero. They
went up to his apartment and he took a shower while
she fixed him some of that Irish coffee they had never
gotten around to the other night. He came out in a terry
cloth robe and sat on the couch beside her. It felt so
right being there with him. They didn't need words to
communicate. A touch, a look, was all it took.

"How did you know where I was?" he asked at last.

"I was coming down to the beach to look for you."

"Why?"

"To show you these." She reached into her bag and
pulled out the photographs she'd received in the mail.
"Jerry, the photographer, sent them to me. I thought
you might enjoy seeing them."

He took them out of the manila envelope and studied them one by one, his face expressionless. "May I
have this one?" he asked, showing her one where her
face was toward the camera and his was hovering close.

"Of course."

He rose and walked over to the shelf where the pictures of his family were scattered. He picked one up,
removed the photo from the frame and slid in the one
he'd just taken from Trish.

She watched him, biting her lip. "I thought you
didn't keep pictures of old girlfriends around," she reminded him.

He came back and sat beside her on the couch, so
close, their shoulders were touching. "You're not an old
girlfriend."

"I see." She wished she could read what he was
thinking behind those dark eyes. Her pulse was starting to beat loudly in her ears and she wasn't sure if it
was because of his nearness, or because she was afraid

to hear the answers to questions—questions that had to be asked. "Then what am I?"

His arm came around her shoulders and began to pull her close. "You're mine, Trish Becker," he said huskily, his eyes soft with feeling. "You're all mine." One hand took hold of her chin. "Do you think you can handle that?"

She nodded her head slowly, drowning in his gaze, unable to look away. If he really meant it . . . "It took me some time to come to my senses," she admitted softly. "But I think I've come to terms with...with the way I feel about you."

A slight smile hovered on his lips and his hand caressed her cheek. "I've missed you, Trish," he told her, his voice calm with sincerity. "Don't go away from me like that again."

She smiled back, so sure of herself all of a sudden. "I won't, Mason," she promised, eyes shining. "Not ever."

He kissed her as though he were drawing life from her lips, and she pressed herself against him, ready to offer him anything he might want, if only it would make him happy. His hands found the hem of her shirt and began to roll it up, revealing soft skin and full breasts.

"Trish," he groaned as he shifted his weight to make it possible to touch more of her. "God, Trish, you make me so crazy."

She felt like a goddess, a symbol of love, stretching to his touch, crying out softly when his fingers rubbed her nipples, helping him shuck away her jeans, and then reaching to yank away the sash to his robe, so that it fell open and revealed his gorgeous body.

He came to her quickly, with an urgency born of denial, his eyes full of hunger, his hands moving feverishly over her body, touching her secret places with a tantalizing suggestion of ecstasy to come. She pulled him to her with as much intensity as he had, crying out his name and digging fingers into his back in the excitement of her need.

"Trish, Trish, I love you," he growled near her ear.

She heard and she smiled, but the heat had built too high to ignore now. She lifted her hips to take him in saying sweet, seductive things, urging him on with her hands, crying out as the wild ride began, savoring it for as long as she could, and then joining him again as he took his turn.

When it was over she lay back exhausted. But his words still echoed in her head. "I love you." Had he really said it? Had he really meant it?

She turned to look at him and whispered them back. "I love you."

He opened his eyes and stared into hers. "Enough to forgive me for quitting?" he whispered back.

"Oh, yes. Enough for that."

He turned fully toward her and pushed her hair out of her eyes with a gentle hand. "Enough to teach me all your surfing secrets?" he asked with a smile.

She grinned. "Absolutely."

His eyes darkened and his hand tightened, grabbing a handful of hair as if to hold on to her, and when he finally spoke again, his voice was rough with emotion. "Enough to marry me?"

Shock tingled through her. "Marry you?" She could hardly believe he'd said the words. Maybe she'd just imagined them.

But he nodded. "I don't want to lose you, Trish. I can't. And I hear that's how you do it. You get married. Then the other person is committed to stay and tough it out with you.''

Her heart was beating so loudly, she could hardly hear what he was saying. But she smiled and touched his cheek, her love in her eyes. ''That's what they say.''

''You want to try it?''

She swallowed. Tears were welling in her eyes. She blinked them back. ''But Mason.... I never thought that you would want to do something like this.''

His smile was self-mocking. ''You mean you never thought a playboy like me would want to tie himself to just one woman? I shared that opinion once upon a time. But you changed my mind.'' He stroked her hair. ''Do you remember that day at the Regatta, when you took me to your secret cove and found the condo being built there? I never saw a woman so open, so honest about her own emotions as you were that day. I think I started falling in love with you there.''

She tried to smile, but the tears were welling again. ''Then it was worth it after all,'' she murmured. ''Mason, I thought I couldn't face giving up my life here but when I stopped and compared that to losing you, I knew I would do anything it took...''

His arms tightened around her. ''You'd change for me? That dreaded word?'' His tone was teasing, but his eyes held nothing but serious intent.

She gazed at him candidly. ''I'd do anything for you, Mason. Anything.''

He held her close, breathing in the scent of her hair. ''You won't have to throw away your life and start over, Trish,'' he told her. Touched by her devotion, his voice was husky. ''I'd do anything for you, too. I'm going to see if I can work things out with your mother. I want to go back to work.''

She drew back and stared at him. "You would do that for me?" she whispered.

He stared back, then kissed her soundly. "I would do that for us," he corrected.

She curled against his chest, her heart singing. "I love you," she murmured happily. "You'll have to give up being a ladies' man, though," she noted as an afterthought.

He sighed with mock despair. "It'll be tough. But I'll even do that." Leaning down, he kissed her nose, her cheeks, her eyelids. "Actually, not so tough," he admitted quietly. "Now I've found you, there's no need to look further."

She tried to laugh. "Ooh, that sounds so cold-hearted!"

He drew her close. "That's me. Old cold-hearted Mason." He kissed her nose. "And that's the way I'm going to be from now on. To everyone but you."

"And the kids," she added tentatively, still blinking back the moisture in her eyes.

He looked surprised. "Do we have kids?" he asked.

She grinned, letting the tears spill down her cheeks. "Not yet," she said shakily. "But we're going to have them soon."

"Good." His hands began to slide down to explore her body once again. "Then we'd better get started." He kissed her neck. "Having kids takes work. Lots and lots of work."

She slipped her arms around his neck and sighed happily. "It's enough to turn me into a workaholic," she murmured.

"You and me both," he agreed, breathing in her scent and sighing with contentment. "You and me both, forever."

"Forever," she echoed. And, looking at the love in his eyes, all her doubts burned away like fog before the summer sun.

Epilogue

The baby kicked and Trish gazed down at her rounded tummy reproachfully.

"Take it easy, little one," she whispered. "I would like to get through Mom and Bert's wedding without giving birth in the aisle."

The baby quieted and she smiled. "What a good little baby," she said, patting her tummy. "If you're half this cooperative once you're out here among us, I'll be a happy mom."

"Are you talking to the squirt again?" Mason entered the room and came up behind where she sat applying last minute touches to her makeup. "Tell him 'hi' for me." He placed his hand on her stomach and smiled as he felt a kick. "This kid's got great legs. He'll be a surfer for sure."

"She," Trish said quietly.

Mason looked startled. "What did you say?"

"She," Trish repeated, her eyes crinkling with teasing humor.

Mason put his ear to the baby. "How do you know? Did it tell you something?"

"No." She reached down and stroked his hair, gazing at him lovingly. "But you've been calling it a 'he' so confidently lately, I just wanted you to remember that girls are nice, too."

"Nice!" Mason rose and kissed her tenderly. "Girls are more than nice," he murmured, nuzzling her neck. "Girls are my very favorite things."

"Straighten your tie," she advised, laughing. "The president of WhiteWaterWaves should look presentable at the wedding of the two company founders, don't you think?"

Mason pulled away reluctantly and did as she advised. Trish watched him with love in her eyes. Everything had worked out so well she hardly dared think about it. Did she deserve this much? Maybe not. But she wanted it all anyway.

Bert and Laura were finally getting married—and about time. It had been two years since they'd started the new surfboard company.

"What do you think is holding them back?" Mason had asked often over the months.

Trish didn't know and didn't venture to guess. She and Mason had planned a quiet wedding themselves, only to find three hundred guests at their reception. Laura liked parties. And the wedding today promised to be big as a circus.

"We've got an hour before we leave for the church," Mason told her. "I've got some calls to make. You rest." He bent to kiss her forehead. "And take care of Junior."

She smiled, watching him leave the room, remembering how she'd once worried that he was too much of a playboy, too full of restlessness, to ever settle down and make a good husband and father. "Wasted time," she murmured to herself. That old Mason had melted away, leaving this new one who was as domesticated as they came.

When Trish looked back over the last two years, she couldn't imagine where the time had gone. When Mason had shown up at WhiteWaterWaves to work things out with Laura and Bert, the two offered him a proposition—take over the company for them while they went on an extended tour of Europe. Mason readily accepted and had things running smoothly and successfully by the time the couple returned. It wasn't long after that when they offered him the presidency. He would be in control and they would take minor roles.

The plan had worked like a charm. Mason was making great boards. The company was one of the fastest growing in the West Coast. And Bert and Laura were traveling and having a wonderful time. Even her father was happy. He'd moved his operation to Carmel and was living like a hermit, happily shaping long boards and ignoring the rest of the world.

Trish sat quietly in the sunlit room thinking about the past and dreaming about the future. Things were very quiet inside her. She put both hands on her rounded stomach and listened, as though she were tuning in to the current of her life. The minutes ticked away.

"Time to go." Mason was back, rushing into the room for his suit coat, then turned to help her up. He stopped when he saw her face. "What is it?"

She smiled at him tremulously. "I think . . . I think we'll make the ceremony," she said, her voice low and husky. "But I'm not too sure about the reception."

"Oh, my God!" He felt her stomach. It was hard as a rock. Their eyes met and they both laughed aloud.

Well, here it was—her chance to bring about the strong family she'd craved all her life. She swallowed hard, looking at her own reflection in the mirror, looking at the reflection of her husband hovering over her. Was she up to the challenge? Was she ready? Was she afraid?

Looking down she stared at her own hand entwined with Mason's, the fingers laced together tightly, forming a bond that looked impossible to break. No, she wasn't afraid. She wasn't doing this alone. And that made all the difference.

"I love you, Mason," she said proudly, her eyes shining with tears.

"I love you, Trish," he murmured back, holding her close. "I love you and I love that little baby you're bringing into the world. I love you both, with all my heart."

That was it—the secret, the key. Thank God she had realized it in time.

*   *   *   *   *

COMING NEXT MONTH

#565 TIME ENOUGH FOR LOVE—Carole Buck
Career blazers Doug and Amy Hilliard were *just too busy*... until they traded the big city winds for the cool country breezes and discovered the heat of their rekindled passion.

#566 BABE IN THE WOODS—Jackie Merritt
When city-woman Eden Harcourt got stranded in a mountain cabin with Devlin Stryker, she found him infuriating— infuriatingly *sexy*! This cowboy was trouble from the word go!

#567 TAKE THE RISK—Susan Meier
Traditional Caitlin Petrunak wasn't ready to take chances with a maverick like Michael Flannery. Could this handsome charmer convince Caitlin to break out of her shell and risk all for love?

#568 MIXED MESSAGES—Linda Lael Miller
Famous journalist Mark Holbrook thought love and marriage were yesterday's news. But newcomer Carly Barnett knew better—and together they made sizzling headlines of their own!

#569 WRONG ADDRESS, RIGHT PLACE—Lass Small
Linda Parsons hated lies, and Mitch Roads had told her a whopper. Could this rugged oilman argue his way out of the predicament... or should he let love do all the talking?

#570 KISS ME KATE—Helen Myers
May's *Man of the Month* Giles Channing thought Southern belle Kate Beaumont was just another spoiled brat. But beneath her unmanageable exterior was a loving woman waiting to be tamed.

AVAILABLE NOW:

#559 SUNSHINE
Jo Ann Algermissen

#560 GUILTY SECRETS
Laura Leone

#561 THE HIDDEN PEARL
Celeste Hamilton

#562 LADIES' MAN
Raye Morgan

#563 KING OF THE MOUNTAIN
Joyce Thies

#564 SCANDAL'S CHILD
Ann Major